Rain Shadow

Published in Canada by Fitzhenry & Whiteside, 195 Allstate Parkway, Markham, ON, L3R 4T8
Published in the U.S. by Fitzhenry & Whiteside, 311 Washington Street, Brighton, Massachusetts 02135

www.fitzhenry.ca   godwit@fitzhenry.ca

We acknowledge with thanks the Canada Council for the Arts, and the Ontario Arts Council for their support of our publishing program. We acknowledge the financial support of the Government of Canada through the Canada Book Fund (CBF) for our publishing activities.

 Canada Council
for the Arts

Conseil des Arts
du Canada

Library and Archives Canada Cataloguing in Publication
ISBN 978-1-55455-341-9 (paperback)
Data available on file

Publisher Cataloging-in-Publication Data (U.S.)
ISBN 978-1-55455-341-9 (paperback)
Data available on file

Text design by Daniel Choi
Cover design by Tanya Montini
Cover image courtesy of Vasin Lee/Shutterstock

Printed and bound in Canada

Rain Shadow

Valerie Sherrard

Fitzhenry & Whiteside

For my granddaughter, Ericka.
Let joy light your way.

Part One

When warm, moist air moves up the side of a mountain, it cools and condenses. These changes in temperature and air pressure trigger rainfall. This happens on what is called the windward side of the mountain, which is generally lush and green with plants and trees.

Before the Beginning

My sister Mira is the sun and I am the moon. That is what she said to me one day. She meant it for mean, like when she tells me she is a jewel and I am a stone or she is a rose and I am a cabbage.

When she says things like that I make a sad face. If I do that she laughs and tells me not to be gloomy because I cannot help being the way I am. Then she goes away and stops buzzing in my ear like an angry bee. The truth is, I do not mind the idea of being a stone or a cabbage.

Jewels are nice with their colour and shine. But I think stones are more interesting. Holding a stone can make you feel peaceful and calm. Some stones are mysterious, with lines and drawings in them. It is a mistake to ever think a stone is not worth looking at.

Or cabbages. Have you seen a cabbage grow from the first tiny leaves all the way to a perfect round ball of green? They are beautiful, and also delicious when Mother cooks them into a boiled dinner, or cabbage rolls or sauerkraut to go with the sausages the butcher makes.

But the moon! Of all the things Mira says I am like that is my favourite one. She is welcome to be the sun if she likes. That is fine with me. The sun has one face for every day. Even on days when the sky is full of clouds, the sun is there behind them, round and orange. It does not change.

The moon is never the same. Sometimes, the moon is a soft white ball, like a curled up kitten. Or it can be yellow or gray as if there is a very pale curtain hanging in front of it. Other times, it is a tiny sliver of light. Daddy says that is like a farmer's scythe, sent to gather a basket of stars. Clouds and trees and other things look mysterious when the moon is behind them. But the best thing of all is the moon's faces. It can smile or frown or look sleepy.

I have even heard the man who tells the weather on the radio talk about the different faces of the moon. Mother told me I was mistaken and that was not what the man said, but I heard him with my own ears. I do not know what Mother's ears heard, or how it could be different from what my ears heard. I asked her, but she told me to go and play and not be under her feet.

Mother never tells my sister to go and play when she asks a question. Mira says that is because she is fourteen years old and almost a grown up woman. Mira says that Mother cannot waste her time explaining things to me because there is no point.

Sometimes Mira says nice things to make me feel better when Mother is angry with me. But other times she makes her voice very, very quiet, so that only I can hear it, and she calls me the thing I do not like to be called, which is Retard.

I am what is called slow. That is why I am in a littler grade at school than other kids who are twelve years old.

Daddy says that I just learn things different from how other people learn.

He says, "Bethany, I think you might surprise a few folks some day."

And he says, "There's no call for one living soul to think they're better than you."

They do think it though—that they are better than me. They think it and sometimes they say it. Only not in those exact words. There are different ways to say things. Sometimes you have to look to see what is hiding *behind* the words.

What I hate the most is when someone talks about me and looks right at me at the same time. It makes me feel like I am a dead bug in a glass case like we saw one time on a class field trip.

I do not talk much myself. It does not seem that I have

a whole lot to say, usually, but that gives me plenty of chance to listen.

I listen very good. I think it might be my talent. Daddy says every last living person has got at least one special talent. It took me a long time to figure out mine because listening good is not a special talent that is easy to spot.

Another thing about me is that I walk with a limp. I do not know if that matters to you or not. It does not matter to me because I am used to it. One of my legs is a little shorter than the other, and that is the reason of the limp.

I think that might be enough to tell you about myself. Mother says it is bad manners to talk about yourself too much. She says that will make people think you are full of yourself. That is one of those things that people say which has another meaning hiding behind it. Of course you are full of yourself. What else would you be full of? What Mother means by this is that people will think you are full of pride.

A girl like me has no cause to be prideful.

I live in Junction, Manitoba. You might have heard of Junction before. Two years ago, in 1947, there was a lot of talk about this place. It went on for a long time. Folks kept saying the same things over and over about what happened.

I did not know much about the girl who was the cause of all the talk. Her name was Gracie and she was in the same grade as my sister Mira. Gracie talked about her hair a good deal but that is not the thing I mostly remember about her. The thing I mostly remember about Gracie is that I took something that belonged to her one day.

It happened during recess. Gracie and some of the other girls were rolling marbles at a plumper on the scuffed place near the side of the school. That is the best place because the grass is gone and the ground is smooth.

When Gracie took her turn, her marble rolled right straight into the plumper. That made her happy. She jumped up and down and clapped her hands. That was when I saw something fly out of the pocket of her skirt. It was shiny, and for a second I thought it was another marble. I looked for it and picked it up only it was not a marble at all. It was a penny, or actually, half of a penny, which is shaped just like half of a moon.

I was checking it over when I heard a voice ask, "What have you got there, Bethany?"

The person who said this was Mira. She was coming toward me with her hand out. Her face was steady and stubborn and I knew she would take the half penny from me. Sometimes Mira takes things she knows I want even if she does not want them herself. I knew she would laugh and say I was touched in the head. She would grab it from me and look it over and hold it up high so I could not reach it. After that she would toss it off in a field, most likely. It would all happen before I could explain that it belonged to the new girl, Gracie, and then it would be too late.

I am not a person to steal. I hope you can take my word for that. One time Mira told all her friends that I took something of hers, which was a lie. It was a silver necklace with three blue beads. It was true that I liked to hold it, but I did not take it. She lost it, probably, and then blamed me. That was the day she threw everything out of my drawers looking for it.

The time I took the half penny was different, because I really did take it. Only, I did not mean to keep it. I would have walked right up to Gracie and passed it back to her if Mira had left me alone. It was her fault that I ran and stumbled and fell and dropped the penny in the grass. I looked for it every recess for the rest of the week but I did not find it and after a while I gave up.

I thought that was the end of that half penny until one day, a long, long time later, I was making a daisy chain. There were lots of daisies in the grassy field next to the playground. That is where I was gathering them when I saw something twinkling on the ground. I squatted down and looked at it and I could hardly believe what I was seeing. It was Gracie's half penny.

I would have given it back to her if I could have, but Gracie was gone then. So, I kept it. That is how I came to take something that belonged to someone else but you should know that was the only time I ever did such a thing.

Chapter One

They were heading north. That was what the man said when he came to our door. He knocked and I went to see who was it and then he asked for the lady of the house. I ran upstairs and told Mother, "Come quick, there is a stranger who wants you."

Mother smoothed her hair and came down the stairs. She opened the door and said, "Yes?" and that is when he told her they were passing through, on their way north.

"I'd be much obliged if you could see fit to let us have some water, ma'am," he said. His face was dusty and he was holding his hat in front of him with both hands.

I looked past him to see who the "us" was. A long blue car was parked in our lane and, sure enough, there was a lady and two boys inside. I put my hand up to wave at them but Mother caught it and gave me a look and I stopped.

"Of course," Mother said to the man. "Tell your family to come in."

"Thank you kindly," said the man. Then he said who his name was and Mother said who her name was. After that, he went to his car and Mother sent me to get Mira.

I found her outside sitting on a tree stump. The tree was gone before I was born but I have seen a picture of it when it was still there. It makes me sad that it got cut down and now all that is left is a stump.

Mira had a book open on her lap but she was not looking at the words.

"Mother wants you," I told her.

"For what?" she asked. "Why can't you do whatever it is?"

"There are strangers who want water," I said.

"Oh *bother!*" Mira said. But she jumped up at once and her face was not cross so I am not sure if she meant it.

Before she went into the house, Mira told me to stay outside.

"Why?" I said.

"Why do you think Mother sent you to get *me*?" she asked. "She doesn't want you in there embarrassing her in front of company."

I pretended not to hear her when she said that. I sat down on the stump like that was what I wanted to do anyway.

A few minutes after Mira went inside, I could hear talking and laughing in the house.

I rocked back and forth a little on the stump.

We hardly ever have strangers at our house. I wanted to go inside where I could see everyone up close, and sort out the jumble of voices. Mostly, I wanted to know more about what they were doing here. Where had they come from and why were they going to this place up north? How old were the boys? What made them decide to come to our house out of all the others along the road?

The sounds of dishes clinking reached me. Then I knew Mother had decided to give them more than water. Probably she had the kettle on for tea. Maybe she and Mira were making sandwiches and piling cookies and slices of lemon roll onto plates.

My stomach grumbled at the thought of the lemon roll. Why should I have to sit out in the hot sun when everyone else was inside talking and eating delicious things?

For one minute, I made myself believe Mira was wrong. Mother would not mind if I went in. I could stand very quiet in a corner.

But I knew I was making a trick on myself. If Mother saw that I had snuck inside, she would frown and tell me to run along and play.

I tried to make myself not care. Daddy says that is what I should do when something makes me sad, but it did not work. I kept right on thinking about how I wanted to be inside to see everybody and hear what they were saying. That is the reason of what I did next.

I crossed over to the house and when I got close to the kitchen window, I went on my knees and crawled until I was beside it. Then I lifted my head up very slow to look inside. It would have been all right, except when I peeked through the bottom part of the window, the man who was a stranger looked right at me.

He put his hand up the way Mother does when she wants me to hush. Only, I do not think he meant it that way because he was smiling. Then, everyone saw his hand up and they looked around and saw me. One of the boys laughed and pointed his finger, which is not polite to do.

"Your other girl is shy, is she?" the lady said to Mother.

"She's not shy, she's—" Mira said. I was glad she saw the look on Mother's face and stopped before she said the rest of it.

I pulled my head back down and crawled as fast as I could go to the corner of the house. When I got there, I stood up and ran behind the barn. I stayed there even after the strangers got back in their car and drove away.

When Mother called out that lunch was ready, I kept on staying where I was. Even the thought of the lemon roll did not change my mind. I stayed there so long I fell asleep and only woke up when Daddy's work was done for the day and our car came rumbling up to the back door.

At supper, Mother and Mira told Daddy about the strangers. That was when I found out that the boys were nine and ten, and they were named Ben and Jonathan. I do not know which one pointed at me and laughed. Anyway, I would still have been his friend if he said he did not mean it.

"They're moving up north," Mira said.

"A little ways past Thompson," Mother added.

I have never been to Thompson. I made a memory in my head to ask Daddy to show it to me on a map later. Daddy is very good at that. He can make a line of the way you to go from Junction to any other place in Manitoba.

"They'll get there just in time for the new school year," Mira said. That made me remember that school will start the week after next. I wondered if the boys I did not get to meet liked school or if they wished that summer would keep on going forever.

"They seemed like a very nice family," Mother said.

But that was before she found out what they left behind.

Chapter Two

"You are not even trying, Bethany!"

I *was* trying, but I did not say that. Mother does not appreciate backtalk. Besides, I knew I had not been quick like she wanted.

"I wish I knew why you are always so disobedient," she said. She took the knife from my hands and her fingers flew across the chopping board, finishing my job.

It was the day after the strangers came to our house and the thing I had been disobedient about was helping with the green beans. That is not a job I mind, but I can never get it done fast enough for Mother. I am quick at trimming off the ends but not at chopping the beans in pieces. If I go fast, some of the round bumps that are inside the beans get cut in half. Maybe that hurts the bean, I do not know, but

\

being careful of them slows me down.

I did not tell Mother the reason of my slowness. That is the kind of thing that she calls foolishness, and she does not like to hear foolishness from me.

"What kind of twelve-year-old child cannot do a simple task like this?" Mother asked, but it was not a question for me to answer. Sometimes Mother asks a question and then answers it herself. That was what she did to this question.

"A slovenly one, that's what kind. I honestly do not know what we are going to do with you, Bethany."

Mother never knew what they were going to do with me. That was a great worry in my head because Mira told me there were Special Places for children like me who have parts that do not work correctly. We are like machines with broken pieces, which click when they should clank, or whirr when they should be silent.

I have never seen one of these Special Places, but Mira said they were dark buildings with bars on the windows. She said the people who worked in these Special Places had long yellow fangs and some of them had terrible, hairy lumps on their faces. Mira said that those were the only kind of people who would work in places with children who were not right in the head.

I did not believe all of Mira's stories. Not like when I was little. But I was never sure which ones were lies. I had been hoping that the Special Places she talked about were made up, but I asked Daddy about them one day.

Daddy said, "There's no need for you to worry about such places, Bethany. You are not going anywhere."

Then I knew the places were real. Even so, Daddy's answer made me feel happy and safe. The next time Mira told me I had better watch out or I would end up in a Special Place, my heart did not even beat funny. I put my chin up and told her Daddy said I was not going anywhere. But Mira laughed.

"Don't be so sure," she told me. "You know very well that Mother *always* works Daddy around to what she wants."

That was true. Daddy *did* give in to what Mother wanted most of the time. Even when he said, "You're not talking me into this one, Inez," in the end she talked him into it just fine.

I did not think Mother would send me to a Special Place for cutting the beans slow. But sometimes a small thing I did wrong was the last straw. (That is not a straw for drinking. It is a kind of straw that gets put on camels when children disobey.)

I am not sure how it worked, exactly, but the last straw always made Mother very angry. She would say, "One of these days, Bethany." Then she would send me out of her sight because she did not want to look at me just then. Only, she never said what was going to happen one of those days and that was a worry to me.

Lucky for me, the telephone rang as Mother was running water over the beans. It was two long rings and that meant the call was for us. After Mother went to answer, I put the forks and knives on the table to be helpful without being asked.

When Mother came back from the phone call her angry face was gone.

"I need you to run an errand," she said. She went to the pantry and got a can of Carnation milk. Then she came out and gave it to me.

"Be a good girl and take this next door to Mrs. Goldsborough."

Of all the things Mother ever asked me to do, going next door was the one I liked the most. Mrs. Goldsborough was very nice and also very interesting. For one thing, she was shrinking. You might think that was not true but she told it to me her very own self one day.

We were in the front room eating gingersnaps and drinking tea. We liked to have tea parties, just the two of us. I was not really drinking tea, but my milk was in a teacup and I was pretending.

"How is your tea, Bethany?" Mrs. Goldsborough asked me. She said it very serious. "Do you need a lump of sugar or a little more milk in it?"

"No, thank you, Mrs. Goldsborough," I said. "My tea is just fine. But can I pass you another gingersnap?"

"You certainly can," Mrs. Goldsborough said. "I've been trying to eat a little more these days. Did you know that I've been shrinking?"

I did not say anything to that. I looked at her careful to see if it was a Really and Truly or not. Then, Mrs. Goldsborough put her teacup down and patted my hand.

"It's true," she said. "I used to be two inches taller and four inches bigger around the middle. Why, if this keeps up, I'll be your size soon."

I did not know if Mrs. Goldsborough had gotten any smaller since she told me that but she had not shrunk down to my size. I thought *that* might be fun but what if she kept right on shrinking after that? I was not quite sure what to think about the matter.

Mrs. Goldsborough was standing in the doorway when I got there with her Carnation milk. She said, "Oh, good, it's you, Bethany."

"I brought Carnation milk," I told her. I held up the can so she could see it.

She reached out and took it from me when I got close enough. "Do you know what I'm going to make with this?"

I am not good at guessing so I shook my head.

"Rice pudding with nutmeg and cinnamon and lovely fat raisins!"

"Mmm!"

"That's what it will be all right. Mmm! But you don't have to take my word for it. I want you to come over tomorrow afternoon and have some with me. Mira can come along too, if she likes."

I told Mother about the invitation as soon as I got home.

"That's very good of her," Mother said. "I can't imagine wanting a bunch of children running in and out of my house when I get to be her age."

"She loves my company," I said. I knew that was true because she told it to me two different times.

"Mrs. Goldsborough is a good neighbour," Mother said, "and a kind woman."

I told Mira about our invitation and the rice pudding. She said, "I might go if there is nothing better to do."

Mira never decided about going to Mrs. Goldsborough's house until it was time to go. It did not seem that Mira liked Mrs. Goldsborough so very much. Not the way I did. But she liked the delicious treats we had there.

I liked it best when Mira had something better to do. On those days I went by myself. It was more fun talking to Mrs. Goldsborough when Mira was not there.

Mira almost decided not to go that day. "Do you know if Mrs. Goldsborough put raisins in the rice pudding?" she asked me.

"Yes. She put nutmeg and cinnamon and lovely fat raisins," I said. Sometimes I can remember things very good.

"I don't like raisins," Mira said. She made a cross face like it was my fault the raisins were going to be there.

"Lovely *fat* raisins," I said.

Mira scrunched her nose. She pushed her shoulders up and down and made a noisy breath.

"I suppose I can put my raisins in your dish," she said. "You'll eat anything."

That was not true. Not at all. Some boys at school tried to get me to eat a stick once and I would not do it even when they told me it tasted like licorice.

But I will eat raisins. So I did not say anything to Mira.

"Come on then," Mira told me. "We might as well go now, since there's nothing else to do."

We walked through the field to Mrs. Goldsborough's house. On the way, I tripped on a lumpy place on the ground and fell. That is easy to happen if one of your legs is shorter than the other one. Mira held her hand out to help me up. Sometimes she only pretended she was helping, and when my hand got close to hers, she yanked it away and laughed. But not that time. She pulled me up and she looked at me in a funny way.

Then she told me the wonderfulest thing I could imagine.

"I have decided something, Bethany. I have made up my mind that I am not going to let anyone pick on you at school this year."

"Really and truly?" I asked.

"Really and truly."

"How will you stop them?"

"I will shake my fist under the nose of anyone who tries, and I will tell them if they want to mess with my sister they will have to mess with me first."

Mira turned to show me the white ball of her fist. She showed me how she was going to shake it. Her face was mean but I did not mind because I knew she was only practising.

That made a happy, floaty feeling inside me. It stayed

there all the rest of the way to Mrs. Goldsborough's house.

We knocked on the door but Mrs. Goldsborough did not come to open it. We did louder and louder knocks. We hollered Mrs. Goldsborough's name.

"Maybe she forgot and went somewhere," Mira said.

But that was not what happened.

Chapter Three

Mira ran out of patience with me when we were walking home from Mrs. Goldsborough's house. That was because I could not stop looking back to see if there was any sign of Mrs. Goldsborough. I was hoping that her face would pop up in the window or a car would drive into her lane and she would get out of it. But those things did not happen.

When we were halfway across the field Mira said, "Okay, Bethany, that's it. You're on your own." After that she went ahead without me. I did not mind because then there was no one to make me hurry up.

I stood and watched Mrs. Goldsborough's house for a little while and when I did that, a feeling came into me that something was wrong.

Daddy says that sometimes feelings are like words.

He says I should listen to what they tell me. That was the kind of feeling this was. It was telling me *go back*. So I listened and went back even though part of me was afraid.

When I got there, I climbed the steps and knocked on the door again. I made a pretend in my head of Mrs. Goldsborough opening the door and smiling and saying, "Well, hello there, Bethany! Come in! Come in!"

But that was only pretend. Mrs. Goldsborough did not come to the door so I tried to think of what to do next. That was when I heard a kitten crying. It sounded like it was inside the house, only that did not make sense because Mrs. Goldsborough does not have a cat.

It was very strange and there was something scary about it too. I listened one more time, as hard as I could. I heard more mewing. That was when I did something bad. I reached my hand up and turned the door knob and opened the door. Not all the way—just enough to see in the hall. I said, "Here kitty, kitty," but the kitten did not come.

I wanted to go inside but I knew Mother would be very, very angry if she found out. So, I closed the door and I went around the house and looked in the windows. That is snooping, which is a very rude thing to do. I did not want to be rude but I could not think of any other way to find the cat.

I stood up on tippy toes to reach the windows, but I still could not see inside. When I got to the door at the front of the house, I knocked on that door and tried to open it. It only moved a tiny bit and then it got stuck. That was when I heard mewing again, only louder and very close.

"Kitty?" I said.

And the kitty answered, "Help me!"

That frightened me so much I jumped backward. I ran down the steps and across the yard and I would have kept going except I tripped on a stone and crashed to the ground.

Falling on my stomach made it hard to breathe. That was scary too, which made me forget about being scared of the talking cat. It is hard to be scared of two things at the same time. I sat up and looked around.

"At least that talking cat is not chasing me." I said this out loud even though nobody else was there. Sometimes talking out loud makes me feel braver. This was a sometime when it worked.

"I am being silly," I said, even louder. "Cats cannot talk."

I got up and watched Mrs. Goldsborough's house for a minute. Something strange was going on. Even though I did not want to, I made myself walk across the lawn and go up the steps again.

I tapped on the door, which was still open a crack. "It is me. Bethany," I said. I meant to say it loud but it came out like a whisper.

"Bethany."

Even though it did not sound like her, I knew that was Mrs. Goldsborough. Then she made a sound like the one that had made me think there was a kitten in there.

I told Mrs. Goldsborough I was coming to help her but I had to go to the other door because this one was stuck. Then I went as fast as I could around to the back of the house. I opened that door and walked in. I knew Mother would not be angry about that because I was helping.

When I went down the hall to the front of the house I saw Mrs. Goldsborough on the floor in front of the stairs that go up to the second floor. She looked very small and crumpled. I started to cry.

Mrs. Goldsborough said, "Stop that!"

I gulped in some big breaths until I wasn't crying anymore.

"Go and phone your mother," she said. Her words came out slow and hard. I think that was because she was hurt. Sometimes when I get hurt I make myself talk with my teeth together to keep from crying. That was what Mrs. Goldsborough sounded like she was doing.

I went to the front room and dialed the telephone. I had to do it two times before it worked and my mother answered.

"Mrs. Goldsborough is hurt," I said. "She is on the floor."

"Dear me," Mother said. "I'll be right there."

After that, a lot of things happened. Mother tried to come in the front door because I forgot to tell her that was where Mrs. Goldsborough was on the floor. When she tried to open the door, it banged on Mrs. Goldsborough and I started to cry again. This time, she did not tell me to stop.

Mother went around to the other door and came down the hall. She shooed me because I was in the way. I went into the kitchen and sat on a chair where I could still see everything. Mother knelt down beside Mrs. Goldsborough. After a minute she went to the phone and I heard her telling someone Mrs. Goldsborough needed an ambulance.

The kitchen smelled like cinnamon and nutmeg. Three glass bowls with spoons sticking out of them were lined up on the counter and I could see that they were full of rice pudding with lovely fat raisins. I knew that one of them was for me. A pain came into my tummy, but I did not know if it was a hungry pain or a different kind of pain.

The ambulance came after a while. The men made loud clomping sounds on the steps but after they came inside the house, they talked quiet and low to Mrs. Goldsborough. When they put her on the stretcher, I squeezed my eyes closed and put my fingers in my ears, but that did not keep out all of the crying sounds she made.

The men took Mrs. Goldsborough through the front door and down the steps. They put her in the ambulance and drove away. Mother came into the kitchen and told me it was time for us to go home. She crossed over to the sink and wet her fingers under the tap. When she was patting water on her face and neck, she saw the empty bowl. She stopped dabbing herself and stared at it.

"Did you eat this dish of pudding, Bethany?"

"My tummy hurt," I said.

"How dare you come into this home and stuff food into your face while a woman is lying on the floor in pain!"

I had only meant to take one tiny bite of the pudding, but it was warm and tasted so good that I forgot to stop. I told Mother I was sorry.

"I doubt that very much," Mother said.

Mother put stretchy plastic on the other two dishes of rice pudding and put them in the fridge. Then she locked Mrs. Goldsborough's doors and we walked home.

On the way, I asked if Mrs. Goldsborough was going to be all right but Mother did not answer.

Chapter Four

"**D**o not coddle that child."

I did not know what that meant, but it was something Daddy did now and then. Mother did not like it. She said if he did not stop I would never learn.

"I'm sure she didn't mean any harm," Daddy said.

"That is hardly the point," Mother told him.

"Bethany, tell your mother you're sorry," Daddy said.

"I'm sorry, Mother," I said.

"Really?" Mother asked. "What are you sorry for?"

"For eating the rice pudding with lovely fat raisins."

"Explain *why* that was wrong," Mother said. When I did not answer she said it two more times, only louder.

"Inez, she's just a child," Daddy said.

Mother put down her teacup and stood up from the table. "It's no wonder she doesn't listen," she told him.

"But Bethany helped Mrs. Goldsborough," Mira said. "Isn't that what really matters?"

"When I want your opinion, Mira, I will ask for it," Mother said. "Now eat your supper. You've barely touched your food."

Then Mother went to the sink and put on the gloves that she wore when she washed dishes. She said they kept her hands from getting dry but I think that was a trick. I know for sure that the gloves really kept her hands from getting wet.

Mira crossed her arms in front of her and slumped down, which was not good posture. She looked over at me and made her eyes move the way she did when she wanted me to help her eat something she did not like.

Most of the things Mira did not like were green, but there was nothing green in that supper. It was leftover roast beef with chopped tomatoes and onions and macaroni all cooked together. That is called a casserole and that was something Mira usually liked to eat. Daddy said Mother whipped up the best casseroles in Junction.

But Mira did not want to eat the leftover roast beef with chopped tomatoes and onions and macaroni. Only, I could not help her because there was never extra room in my tummy when Mother was angry with me.

After a while, Mira said, "I don't feel good."

"Check her forehead," Mother said. Daddy leaned

across the table and put the back of his hand on Mira's head.

"She does seem a little warm," Daddy said.

Mother checked, too, and then she went and got the thermometer and stuck it under Mira's tongue. After a few minutes, she took it out and squinted at it.

"Just over one hundred," Mother said. "It looks like you're coming down with something."

"It better be gone before school starts," Mira said. "I *can't* miss the first day!"

That might make you think Mira loved school but that was not the reason of her wanting to be there the first day. One reason was she had a smart new outfit she could not wait to show off. That was the exact thing she told me.

The other reason was that she loved a boy named Alex Filmon. I heard her whispering about him to Sharon Goldrick one day when Sharon and her mother were visiting. Mira said that she did not know how she could wait until the first day of school to see Alex again because she was crazy in love with him.

"School doesn't start for another five days," Mother said. "I'm sure you'll be fine by then. In fact, you'll probably be right as rain by morning. But for now, you need to go brush your teeth and get ready for bed."

I felt sorry for Mira, that she had to go to bed so early. After a while I decided to go upstairs to see if she wanted a drink of water. But Mother was there, and she came to the doorway and put her hands on my shoulders to stop me from going in.

"We don't need both of our girls getting sick," Mother said. Then she bent down and kissed me on the top of my head. "Why don't you go and do some colouring for a while?"

Colouring was something I was extra good at. I did as Mother said and coloured a picture of a girl holding a puppy. When I was finished, I did my best printing and wrote TO MIRA on it. After that I asked Daddy to cut the page out of the book.

Mother saw it on the table when she came downstairs. She picked it up and said it was sure to help cheer Mira up. Then she said I could have a cookie for being such a good sister.

When it was my bedtime, I tiptoed past Mira's room but she was not asleep. She called out, "Thanks for the picture, Bethany!"

"Did it cheer you up?" I said.

"Yes."

"Do you feel better now?"

"No. My throat hurts," she said.

"I wish it would stop," I told her.

"Me too."

When I said my prayers, I did an extra God bless for Mira. The first one was the God bless Mira I do every night, except when I am sleepy and I forget my prayers. The second one was for her throat to not hurt.

But in the morning Mira still had a sore throat.

"This is the second time this year," Mother said. "We

should have had her tonsils taken out years ago."

"Is she too old for that now?" Daddy asked.

"I don't think so," Mother said. "But Doctor Mynarski said we should wait, remember? He said lots of children grow out of sore throat problems."

After breakfast, Mother sent Daddy to Clive's General Store to get some popsicles for Mira's throat and I got to go along for the drive.

I loved going in the car with Daddy. We liked to sing and when there was no one else with us, we sang as loud as we wanted. We sang two songs on the way to Clive's General Store. The first one was called *I'm Looking Over a Four Leaf Clover* and I knew all the words perfect. Every time we got to the part that said, "somebody I adore," Daddy pointed at me and that meant *I* was somebody he adored.

The second song we sang was called *Buttons and Bows*. The words were harder in that song but I liked singing it anyway because it made me feel like bouncing from side to side. I was allowed to do that when it was only me and Daddy in the car.

When we got to Clive's General Store and went inside, Daddy said what he always said, which was, "Hello, hello!"

And Clive, who is Mr. Finkbeiner to me, said, "Hello yourself," which was what he always said back.

There were three people at the counter plus Mr. Finkbeiner. Mrs. Laidlaw was one of them and she looked over and nodded to Daddy. Then she saw me. And that was when something happened that never happened to me before.

Mrs. Laidlaw said, "Well, look who's here. It's Bethany Anderson. The girl who rescued Mrs. Goldsborough!"

Then Mrs. Laidlaw and Mr. Finkbeiner and the others who were at the counter clapped their hands. They clapped and clapped, and they said things like, "Three cheers for Bethany," and "What a girl!"

When they were finished clapping they kept smiling at me. I felt very, very happy inside. Then Mr. Finkbeiner gave me a penny candy bag full of butterscotch drops for free and Mrs. Laidlaw gave me a nickel.

I remembered my manners and said, "Thank you for the candy, Mr. Finkbeiner. And thank you for the nickel, Mrs. Laidlaw."

They both said I was very welcome. After that, Daddy bought the popsicles and we drove right straight home and put them in the freezer so they would not melt.

I dumped the butterscotch drops from Mr. Finkbeiner out on the kitchen table and made them into two piles. One pile had six and one pile had five so I ate one and then both piles had five.

"What have you got there, Bethany?" Mother asked when she came into the kitchen.

I told her everything about what happened at Clive's General Store.

"I see," Mother said.

"So I made two piles of candies," I said. "One for me and one for Mira."

"You're a good girl," Mother said. "I'll take them up to her in just a bit."

I hoped that the butterscotch drops might help poor Mira feel better, but her throat was still sore the next day.

Part Two

As clouds move to the other side of the mountain, the sinking air compresses and warms. The rain stops and the dried air picks up moisture from the ground. The dry area on the downwind, or leeward, side of the mountain is called a rain shadow. The rain shadow area is typically arid with very little plant life.

Chapter Five

When Mrs. Goldsborough finally came back home, she had a big white cast on her leg because the bone got broken in two places.

I saw her get out of a car and go into her house. It took her a long time because she was walking with a crutch. A lady I did not know was helping her but that did not speed her up. Daddy said the lady's name was Miss Kerr and she was going to stay with Mrs. Goldsborough and take care of her until the cast was ready to come off.

I pressed my nose against the kitchen window and wished I could go over there. I wanted to ask Mrs. Goldsborough how she was feeling. But I was not allowed to go there. I was not allowed to go anywhere. Nobody in our house was.

The reason of that was a phone call we got from the

man who came here with his family on their way up north a few weeks ago. Daddy answered the phone and I could see he was surprised. He smiled and waved to Mother to come over beside him.

"It's real nice of you to call," Daddy said. "Inez told me about meeting your family and I was sorry I wasn't here at the time. I imagine you're settled into your new house by now. How are things going?"

After that Daddy mostly listened to the man talking. He stopped smiling and he hardly said anything for a few minutes. Then he said, "Oh?" and listened some more and said, "I see," two times, and after a bit he said, "I'm sorry to hear it."

"What is it?" Mother asked. Daddy held up his pointing finger which means to not say anything for one minute.

That was when Daddy said, "Our oldest girl, Mira, has had a fever and sore throat for a couple of days. But that's not unusual for her."

Mother made a strange little sound. She put her hand over her mouth and took a step backward, away from Daddy, and sat down on the brown chair with big arms.

"Yes, certainly—we'll have the doctor in as soon as he can come," Daddy said. "I, that is, my wife and I appreciate the call. I hope your boy will be all right."

After Daddy put the phone down, he went and stood beside the chair where Mother was sitting. He took her hand but Mother pulled it back. She put both of her hands over her ears and said, "No," very loud.

"Their son," Daddy said, "the younger one—"

"Stop!" Mother cried. "I don't want to hear it."

Daddy stopped talking. He stood there while Mother shook her head back and forth over and over. After she finished doing that, she took a big breath and looked up at Daddy's face.

"Their boy has polio, doesn't he?" she said.

"Yes," Daddy said. "But that doesn't mean Mira—"

"Of course it doesn't," Mother said. She jumped up. "Call Doctor Mynarski. Right now. He'll tell us—it's her tonsils, just like always. That's all it will be."

Daddy got the phone book out and looked up the number and called like Mother had told him to. A little while later Doctor Mynarski drove in. Mother was watching for him and she opened the door when he was still getting out of his car.

"Thank you for coming," she told him as he passed her his hat. "I'm sure it's just the usual thing—you know how prone Mira is to tonsillitis. But under the circumstances—"

"Of course, of course," Doctor Mynarski said. "Better safe than sorry. Now, where's our patient?"

Mother wanted to go to Mira's room with him, but Doctor Mynarski said she and Daddy should wait downstairs. They sat down on the couch in the front room.

I was across the hall in the dining room, where we ate if there was company or a special occasion. Sometimes I liked to sit in the chair with arms at the end of the table and pretend I was a grown up lady, but not that day. That day, I was not in a mood for pretending. I was in a mood for hearing what was going on in the front room.

I could hear Daddy tapping his foot on the floor. Mother asked him to please stop it but after a moment he forgot and started to tap again. Then Mother said she was being a nervous Nellie and Daddy said why didn't she put on a pot of tea.

So, Mother went into the kitchen. I peeked around the corner to see if Doctor Mynarski was coming down the stairs yet and then I went across the hall to the archway of the front room. Daddy was sitting very still.

"My tummy feels strange," I said.

Daddy's head jerked up and he made a funny sound. Then he said, "Goodness, Bethany, you startled me."

"Sorry, Daddy."

"No, no. You didn't do anything wrong." Daddy put his hand out to me. "Come on over here."

I went and stood in front of him.

"Did you say you were feeling sick?" he asked. He touched my cheek and forehead.

"Not like throwing up," I said. "My tummy feels scared."

"So does mine, angel," Daddy said. He hugged me and patted the spot beside him on the couch. "Come and sit up here with me."

After a minute Mother came back. She sat on the other side of me. She put her arm around my shoulder and pulled me close to her. That made my tummy feel a little bit better.

But it did not last long because Doctor Mynarski came down the stairs and into the room. Mother and Daddy both stood up quick so I stood up quick too. We all looked at Doctor Mynarski. He cleared his throat.

"Hello, Bethany," he said. "How would you like to do me a little favour?"

"Okay," I said.

"Would you go into the kitchen while I talk to Mommy and Daddy?"

Mother began to cry then. She sat back down on the couch and put her hands over her face. When I started to walk to the kitchen like Doctor Mynarski wanted, Mother was saying, "No, no, no, no, no," over and over.

The kitchen is not a good place for hearing people talking in the front room—not like the dining room. I could not tell what words Doctor Mynarski was saying but it was not hard to figure out it was something bad.

It felt like I waited a very long time. Finally, Mother came into the kitchen and turned off the burner where the teapot was. I heard Daddy talking quiet to Doctor Mynarski and then the front door closed and Daddy came into the kitchen too.

"Bethany," Daddy said.

"Yes, Daddy?"

"Your sister is very ill. She has something called polio."

"Is that why her throat is sore?"

"Yes. And Mira is going to have to go to Winnipeg, and spend some time in the hospital."

"How much time?"

"We don't know that yet."

"Until she gets better?" I asked.

"Yes, until she's well enough to come back home," Daddy said.

"Marian May was in the hospital for two weeks when she got her suspendix out. Is Mira getting her suspendix out too?"

"Appendix. And no, Mira is sick in a different way."

"Bethany," Mother said, "Would you go out to the garden and pick some peas for me?"

I took the basket Mother gave me and went out the back door but I did not go right to the garden. I stood very still by the door and I heard Mother tell Daddy she was going with him to Winnipeg and that was all there was to it.

"Who's going to take care of Bethany?" Daddy asked. "You know she can't come with us."

"I'll find someone," Mother said. Then she started to cry again, and I walked quick to the garden and picked peas.

When the basket was almost full I brought the peas into the kitchen. Mother was talking on the phone. She said, "Excuse me one second, Laura," and put her hand over the phone and told me, "Get a bowl, then go to the front step and shell those. That's a good girl."

I went back outside but I disobeyed Mother about

going to sit on the front step. I sat on the ground beside the back step and listened again. I wanted to hear who Mother was getting to take care of me when they took Mira to the hospital in Winnipeg.

I could not hear everything, but I could tell that Mother made a lot of phone calls. She was not having much luck even though she said, "Please," a lot of times.

Then Mother put down the phone and said a bad word and I went to the front step with the peas.

It takes a long time to get peas out of the shells. I was only finished about half of them when Mother came out the front door and said, "Bethany, you are going to have a babysitter when your father and I take Mira to the hospital."

"Who?"

"Mrs. Melchyn."

"I do not want her," I said. "She is always crabby."

"Do not speak about your elders that way, Bethany. And Mrs. Melchyn is not crabby. She may be *firm*, but there is nothing wrong with that." Mother told me. "And I don't want to hear any more backtalk about it. I was lucky to find anyone at all."

I put my head down and squeezed open another pod. I pushed the peas into the bowl and did not say any more backtalk, but I did not like the idea of having Mrs. Melchyn around. Not one bit.

Chapter Six

Mrs. Melchyn came the next morning.

"I can't tell you how grateful we are," Mother said.

"I'm not afraid of a few germs," Mrs. Melchyn said, settling into a chair at the kitchen table. "Besides, I never get sick. I have the constitution of a horse."

I saw that she had a big suitcase with her.

"Are you going on a holiday?" I asked.

"A holiday? Of course not—I'm here to take care of you."

"But why did you bring your suitcase?"

"Doctor Mynarski has quarantined our house for twenty-one days," Mother said. "Mrs. Melchyn will have to stay here until that's over."

"Is that more than a week?" I asked. Numbers are hard for me but I know about weeks. A new one starts

ELDER

every time I go to Sunday School.

"It's three weeks," Mrs. Melchyn said.

Three weeks with crabby Mrs. Melchyn around did not sound good to me.

"It's very kind of Mrs. Melchyn to leave her own home for so long to help us," Mother said. "You be a good girl for her and do what you're told."

"I will."

That was when we heard Daddy coming down the stairs. He was going slow because he was carrying Mira. Her face was pink and sleepy. When they got to the bottom step, Mother gave me a kiss and a very fast hug.

"I guess we're off," she said.

"Can I go tell Mira goodbye?" I asked.

"It's best if you don't get too close, just in case," Mother told me.

"Mira!" I called. "I cannot get too close, just in case, but I am blowing you a very big kiss!"

I blew the kiss and Mira put her hand up to catch it.

"Did you get it?" I asked.

Mira's mouth moved but no sound came out.

"She said she did," Daddy told me. Then he carried her out the front door and Mother went behind with some bags and they all got in the car and drove away.

I looked at Mrs. Melchyn and Mrs. Melchyn looked at me. It was like the game where you lose if you look away first. But not really because I do not think Mrs. Melchyn plays games.

After a minute, Mrs. Melchyn said, "Why don't you go

and play in your room or outside until lunch, Bethany?"

I went to my room but it was not to play. I had remembered a day at school when Lawrence Philpot's older sister Sheila brought a penny for show and tell. Sheila told us her penny was lucky because she found it on the ground. She said that luck comes out when you rub it.

There was an old shoebox in the corner of my closet. That was where I put things which are called odds and ends. The piece of Gracie's penny was in there and I picked it up and rubbed and rubbed for a long time. Sheila said it only takes a few minutes to let the luck out, but I rubbed it longer because half of a penny might only be half as lucky.

After that, I went outside but I did not feel like playing. So, I pushed the wheelbarrow to the front yard and got in it to watch the road in front of our house. That was not much fun but sometimes it was better than nothing when there was no one to play with.

A few cars and trucks went by. One car looked like ours but it was somebody else's. I waved to everybody, even if I did not know them, and everybody mostly waved back. Then I got sleepy and my hand felt too heavy to wave.

Lunch was a grilled cheese sandwich and four slices of cucumber. Mrs. Melchyn told me I was a good girl for finishing everything.

"I can't abide a picky eater," she said. "Now, would you like to help me with the dishes?"

"No, thank you," I said.

Mrs. Melchyn looked surprised and angry. But after a minute her face changed and she laughed.

"Well, help me anyway," she said. "I'll wash and you can dry."

I went to the sink and got the cloth.

"So, Bethany," Mrs. Melchyn said as she turned on the tap, "you're having an extra long summer holiday."

"Yes, because of the quarantine," I said.

"And do you miss seeing your classmates?"

"Only the ones who are nice to me," I said.

"Are some of them unkind?"

"I am not supposed to be a tattletale," I said.

Mrs. Melchyn washed our plates and put them in the drain tray. "My husband was born with a cleft palate," she said. "When he was a boy, other children were sometimes unkind to him because of it."

"Did I ever see your husband?"

"No. He died a long time before you were born."

Mrs. Melchyn did not say anything else after that. I wondered if she was crabby because her husband died but I did not ask her in case that was rude.

When the dishes were finished I went outside and watched some more cars. The school bus came after a while. Lawrence Philpot was looking out the window. When he saw me, he stuck his tongue out, poked his thumbs into his cheeks, and wiggled his hands beside his face. That was not polite.

Sometimes Lawrence is my friend. One day I dropped

my eraser and he picked it up and put it back on my desk. Another time he broke off a piece of his banana and gave it to me. But he is not my friend when he pulls my braids or makes faces.

If our teacher, Mr. Wolnoth, sees Lawrence or anyone being rude he makes them stand up and apologize. That means say sorry.

Our school has nine grades. The older students sit at the back of the room and some of them stick up for me if they see things that Mr. Wolnoth does not. One time Benjamin Pederson drew an ugly face and wrote my name on it and Luke Haliwell said he had better knock it off if he knows what's good for him. Another time, Eva Yuen told two girls that they could never borrow her fan again because they called me the thing I do not like to be called.

The two friends I like the best are Mary Haig and Lizzie Newmarch. We play hopscotch and skip rope. I go to their houses when they have a birthday and they come to my house when I have one. And sometimes we go to each other's houses just to play and visit. That is not too often because it is too far to walk and somebody needs to drive us. Mary and Lizzie never call me names or say mean things or tell me I am too dumb to read.

I had learned to read a little bit, but not enough to have a turn at reading out loud in class. When Mr. Wolnoth says who he wants to stand up and read, he never says my name. On Parent Night, he told my mother the reason of that was so the others will not know and I will not be embarrassed.

The only problem was everybody already knew about it. In the playground sometimes, other kids would come up to me and say, "You can't even read, Bethany."

Then I would tell them that I do not care because I do not want to read, but that was not true. I love books and stories. I wished I did not always have to wait for someone to read to me. I thought it would be the wonderfulest thing in the world if I could read to my own self.

Every time I said, "Star Light, Star Bright," that was the thing I wished for. I was not sure if it would work but I was not giving up. Daddy always said I should never give up because one day I would even surprise myself.

Chapter Seven

It was getting dark outside when Daddy got home from Winnipeg. He was all by himself.

"Where is Mother?" I said when he came into the house.

Daddy put his hat on the table and pulled out a chair. When he sat down, he patted his knee for me to come and sit with him.

"The doctors said it would be a good idea for Mommy to stay in Winnipeg with Mira for a few days."

"Okay," I said.

"Did you behave yourself today?"

"I think so. Did I, Mrs. Melchyn?"

"She was fine," Mrs. Melchyn said. "How long will your wife be staying in Winnipeg?"

"We don't know just yet. Until the doctors know a little more about Mira's condition."

"And where will Inez stay while she's there?" Mrs. Melchyn asked.

"The mother of another little girl with polio invited her to stay at their home."

Mrs. Melchyn frowned. She said, "I don't trust people who do things for complete strangers."

"How come?" I asked.

"I was speaking to your father," she told me. "Children should not be giving opinions or asking questions in the middle of an adult conversation."

Then Mrs. Melchyn told me it was time to get ready for bed so I did not find out why she did not trust the lady who let Mother stay at her house.

It was hard to fall asleep that night. The house felt strange with Mira and Mother away and Mrs. Melchyn sleeping in the guest bed in Mother's sewing room.

Daddy was already gone to work when I got up in the morning. Mrs. Melchyn gave me Red River cereal for breakfast. It was lumpy and getting cold and did not taste the way it tasted when Mother made it.

I started to eat it anyway because I remembered that Mrs. Melchyn does not like children who are picky. It was not easy but I swallowed two bites and took another one. That was when my eyes started to get full of tears.

I put my head down so Mrs. Melchyn would not see the tears but that was not the only problem. I could not swallow the cereal in my mouth no matter how hard I tried. After a minute I ran upstairs to the bathroom.

I spit the cereal in the toilet and finished crying. After that, I washed my face with cold water like Mother showed me to do if I have been crying and I do not want anyone to know.

I did not seem to know why that cereal made me cry.

When I went back downstairs I told Mrs. Melchyn I did not want to eat the cereal.

"It's very wrong to waste perfectly good food," Mrs. Melchyn said. "There are children starving in other parts of the world."

I did not know what to say about that.

"I will make you a piece of toast this time," Mrs. Melchyn said, "but you mustn't be wasteful again."

I made a promise in my head that I would eat the Red River cereal the next time but Mrs. Melchyn did not make it for my breakfast any other day.

It was very boring with Mira and Mother away. Daddy was busy with his work every day and Mrs. Melchyn did not like to play checkers or Old Maid or any of the games some grownups play with me.

Mrs. Melchyn only liked to make meals and clean the house. Sometimes after supper she sat on the couch and knitted socks and fell asleep. If I fall asleep on the couch Daddy carries me up to bed. He did not have to carry Mrs. Melchyn, though, because after a while her eyes opened and she shook her head and went right back to knitting.

I helped with the dishes and if she needed something and did not know where Mother kept it, I showed her where it was. The rest of the time she told me to go outside or find something to do to entertain myself or read a book.

I never told Mrs. Melchyn that I did not really know how to read. Sometimes I got out a book that Mira gave me a long time ago. It was her favourite book before she got too old for it, and it was my favourite when I wanted to practice reading. That book was called *Make Way for Ducklings*. I could not read very many of the words but I still loved to look at the pictures.

The first week that Mira was in the hospital Daddy went to Winnipeg to see her and Mother two times. I wanted to go too but when I asked, Daddy said, "Not this time."

Daddy had a list of things to take to Mother. I helped him find them and put them in a bag.

I did not get to go with Daddy the week after that either but I did not give up. I asked again the next time.

"You would be bored on the long drive," Daddy said.

"I am bored staying here with Mrs. Melchyn," I told him.

"It's just not possible," Daddy said. "I can't take you into the hospital, and I can't leave you in the car the whole time I'm in there."

"I will be a good girl," I promised. "I do not mind waiting in the car."

"I'm sorry, Bethany but you can't come with me."

Daddy squatted down and put out his arms to give me a hug but I did not want one. I yelled, "No!" and pushed him as hard as I could with both hands. That made him fall backward. He looked like he was going to crabwalk. That probably sounds like it was funny but it was not.

I stood very still. When Daddy got up he shook his head and said, "Don't be like that, Bethany. I have to go. Now come give your old dad a kiss and hug goodbye."

I did not answer.

Daddy waited for a minute. He kept looking at me. Then he said, "All right, I guess I'll see you when I get back."

I crossed my arms in front of me and Daddy picked up the bag of things he was taking to Mother and went out the door.

As soon as the car started to drive out to the road I changed my mind. I ran after it calling for Daddy to stop but the car kept going.

My heart started to hurt. I wished I had given Daddy a hug and kiss goodbye.

Mrs. Melchyn told me I had been a wicked girl. "What if your father never came back?" she said. "That would be the last memory you ever had with him."

"Daddy *is* coming back," I said.

"I suppose that's not something you can grasp," Mrs. Melchyn said. "Well, you might as well run along and find something to do until lunch."

I tried to find something to do but I was not in the mood to play. My insides felt sad all day, until Daddy came home again.

When our car finally came in the driveway I could see that Mother was with Daddy. I ran over and looked in the backseat. Mira was not there.

"Is Mira coming home soon?" I asked when Mother got out of the car.

"Not for a while," Mother said. "And I'm just here for the night. Your father is taking me back first thing in the morning."

"And you can come for the drive this time," Daddy said. "Mommy can stay with you while I go see Mira."

I was very glad of that but I did my best not to look excited in case that hurt Mrs. Melchyn's feelings.

Chapter Eight

Mrs. Melchyn was in the kitchen when I went downstairs in the morning.

"Would you like a scrambled egg for breakfast?" she said.

"With ketchup?"

"If you like."

"Yes, please," I said. "Are Mother and Daddy still sleeping?"

"I'm afraid not," Mrs. Melchyn said. "They were called to the hospital during the night."

I stared at her.

"Your sister took a bad turn."

"Daddy said I could go with him this time."

"Yes, but he couldn't wait for the morning," Mrs. Melchyn said. "He had to go when the hospital called."

She got an egg out of the fridge and cracked it into a bowl.

"He *said*."

Mrs. Melchyn beat the egg with a fork. "Things don't always turn out the way we'd like them to," she said. She added a bit of milk to the bowl, beat it some more, and poured it into the frying pan.

I did not care what Mrs. Melchyn said—it was not fair. But I did not talk back because I did not want to get sent to my room and miss out on my scrambled egg.

Mrs. Melchyn put the ketchup on top of the egg instead of beside it for dipping like Mother does. It was still delicious and I was almost finished eating when I heard a car coming up our driveway. When I peeked out the window, I saw that it was our car.

Mrs. Melchyn came to the window, too. She said, "Oh, dear."

"They came back for me!" I told her. I jumped up and down and clapped my hands.

"Bethany, please sit down for a moment," Mrs. Melchyn said.

But I could not make myself do that. I raced out the door and ran to the car as fast as I could.

"Thank you, thank you, Daddy!" I yelled. "Thank you for coming back for me!"

The car was turned off already but Daddy and Mother did not get out. They sat very still, looking down.

Mrs. Melchyn came out the front door and down the steps. She said, "Come back inside with me, Bethany."

"I'm waiting for Mother and Daddy," I said.

Mrs. Melchyn walked over and took my hand. She tried to pull me toward the house.

"No!" I yelled. I knew I would be in trouble but I did not care.

Then Daddy opened his door. "It's all right," he said. "I'll speak with her."

Mrs. Melchyn let go of me and Daddy got out of the car. His face did not look right.

"Did you come back to get me, Daddy?"

"Just a moment, Bethany," Daddy said. He went around the car and opened up Mother's door. Mother did not move, so Daddy put his hand out and after a minute she took it and held onto it while she got out.

I said, "Hello, Mother," very quiet. Mother did not answer. She was looking at Daddy and suddenly she fell against him and began to make a strange noise.

"Is Mother sick?" I said. One time, I got sick from being in the car too long.

"Bethany, please come inside with me," Mrs. Melchyn said. Daddy nodded at me, and this time I obeyed.

When we were in the living room, I asked Mrs. Melchyn, "Do you think Mother got polio like Mira?"

"No, Bethany. Just sit quietly until your mom and dad come in."

I sat down on the couch and Mrs. Melchyn sat in a chair across from me. It felt like a long time before Mother and Daddy came in. Mother went right upstairs but Daddy came into the living room where I was waiting. He sat down beside me on the couch, but sideways so he was facing me. Mrs. Melchyn stood up.

"I'll be in the kitchen," she said. "Please let me know if there's anything you need."

Daddy whispered something I could not hear and she went out of the room. I heard her shoes clacking down the hall. Then a kitchen chair scraped on the floor. Daddy leaned forward.

He said, "I have something very sad to tell you."

I waited but Daddy did not tell me the sad thing right away. He took a big breath that made his shoulders go up and down and he put his hand on my knee.

Then he said the terrible thing.

"Your sister has died, Bethany."

Did you ever hear something inside your head again and again even if the person only said it one time? That was what happened to me with the terrible thing that Daddy said. The words sounded wrong and strange and far away, as if Daddy was saying them over and over through a cardboard tube. But even though I kept hearing them, they did not make sense.

It was like sometimes at school when Mr. Wolnoth tells me something and I do not know what he means even if I understand the words.

I stood up.

"Mira is in the hospital in Winnipeg," I said. Because maybe Daddy forgot or got mixed up. "The doctors are making her better."

Daddy shook his head.

"They did everything they could but they couldn't save her," Daddy said.

"No," I said. Daddy did not answer, so I said it again. I said it louder and louder.

After that Daddy put his arms out like he wanted to hug me.

"It will be all right," he said.

I yelled, "NO!" one more time, very loud and long. Then I punched him. It scared me a little bit but Daddy did not look angry, only surprised. So I did it again and again. I could not stop. I kept on punching faster and faster until suddenly I felt weak and floppy like a rag doll.

After that I started to cry and even after all the punches I did to him, Daddy hugged me until I was finished.

Chapter Nine

Mira was in the living room. She was in a white coffin, up on the table where Mother usually puts plants that need lots of sun. Mira had on the velvet dress she wore when her Sunday School class sang *O Little Town of Bethlehem* at the Christmas program last winter.

It looked like she was sleeping. Her eyes were closed and she was very still. Also, she was holding her hands together. But Daddy told me she was not really there. He said that Mira left her body and went to heaven. She did not need her body there.

Mother told me to kiss Mira's cheek. I did it but I did not like it. I hoped Mother would not make me do it again. Mira's body felt cold and strange without Mira in it.

Mrs. Melchyn was still at our house. I heard her tell Mother she would stay for the first day of the wake even though the quarantine was over. I went to see if it was true, and the orange quarantine paper that had been in the window was gone.

"Is the quarantine over because Mira died?" I asked Daddy.

"No. Yesterday was the last day," Daddy said. He put two fingers over his mouth and closed his eyes very tight.

I was going to ask if I could go visit Mrs. Goldsborough but when Daddy opened his eyes again he told me Mother wanted to see me upstairs. I went up and knocked on the bedroom door.

"Come in."

I pushed the door enough to stick my head inside. "Did you want me, Mother?"

"Yes. Come here, dear." Mother patted the spot on the bed beside her.

"I need you to be an extra good girl today," Mother said. "There will be a lot of people coming to pay their respects to your sister, and you must be on your best behaviour."

"Yes, Mother."

"That means no running about or talking loudly. Do not speak unless you are spoken to. Some visitors will tell you they are sorry about your sister. You tell them thank you. Nothing more unless they ask you a question. Can you remember that?"

"Yes, Mother."

"That's a good girl. Go and put on your navy dress. I've laid it out on your bed."

I got dressed like Mother told me to. After that she brushed my hair and tied it back with a piece of dark ribbon.

"Be sure you stay clean," she said. "Now, go and see if you can help Mrs. Melchyn with anything."

Mrs. Melchyn had been busy. She had baked banana bread and lemon cookies and two kinds of squares. I helped her put them on plates and she covered them with plastic wrap. Then she got out the cups and saucers Mother used when there was company and set them on the dining room table with the sweets.

Mother got Daddy to move all of the dining room chairs into the living room.

"There are only ten places for guests to sit, even with the extra chairs," she said. "That won't be nearly enough."

"People can stand," Daddy said.

But nobody had to stand. Only a few people came to our house and some of them did not even come inside. They brought food and cards and said they were sorry for our loss. Then they went away.

Just two people sat down in the room but they did not stay very long. They both told me they were sorry about my sister, just like Mother had told me they would. I said, "Thank you," in my quiet voice. I did not run around the house even though it was hard sitting on a chair all afternoon.

I was glad when we stopped doing the wake and went to the kitchen to eat supper. The room smelled good from the sliced ham and potato scallop and coleslaw and biscuits on the table. Mother stared at it and then pushed her chair back and walked away.

"You need to keep your strength up, Inez," Daddy said but Mother went upstairs without answering.

Mrs. Melchyn reached over and cut up the piece of ham on my plate. I took a bite before I remembered to tell her thank you and then I could not do it because it is not polite to talk with food in your mouth. But Mrs. Melchyn did not remind me or even frown at me. She looked over at Daddy.

"If you need me to stay for a few more days, I can certainly do that," she said.

"That's very kind of you," Daddy said, "but we'll be all right. Anyway, I expect you'll be glad to get back to your own home."

Mrs. Melchyn dabbed at her mouth with a napkin. "If you're sure," she said, "I'll go after the wake ends this evening. But I'm only a phone call away if you need me again."

Mother came back downstairs after a while. She had a cup of tea and two tiny bites of a biscuit. After that, Mrs. Melchyn cleared the table and shooed us back to the living room.

"I feel sure there will be a good crowd tonight," she

said. "A lot of folk would have been at work this afternoon."

Mrs. Melchyn was wrong. There was no crowd at all—only a few people now and then. Nobody sat down.

Everybody who came told Mother and Daddy they were sorry but they could not stay. Then they said the reasons they had to leave. Daddy said, "We understand," every time.

Aunt Edith and Uncle Harold came for a few minutes. They cried and hugged Mother and Daddy and me. They said if there was anything they could do, to be sure to let them know. But they could not stay either.

After a while I got sleepy. Mother was very disappointed in me. She said that people would think I did not care about my sister if I could not even stay awake for one evening. After that, every time my eyes started to close, I pinched my leg as hard as I could. It helped me stay awake and I did not even care how much it hurt.

After it was over, Mrs. Melchyn said she would be going.

"Bethany, do you have anything you want to say to Mrs. Melchyn?" Mother asked.

When Mother asks me that, it is to remind me to tell someone thank you.

"Thank you for taking care of me, Mrs. Melchyn," I said.

Mrs. Melchyn patted my head. I did not like that but I did not complain. She told me I was a good girl, and said, "I know you'll be a great comfort to your parents in the days to come."

Daddy carried her suitcase to her car and then she drove away. When he came back into the house, Mother told him, "Did you see that, Jack? Your own sister wouldn't even sit down with us—not even for ten minutes."

Daddy did not answer. He opened his hands and held them out, like he was showing her he had nothing hidden in them.

"Where was everyone?" Mother said. Red spots popped out on her pale face. "Where are all our friends? It's like Mira didn't matter."

"You know that's not true, Inez," Daddy said. "People are afraid."

"The quarantine is over," Mother said. She sat down and hugged herself. Then she bent in half and cried.

After a minute Daddy put a hand on her shoulder and said, "We'd better try to get some sleep. Tomorrow will be another long day."

"Go ahead," Mother said. "I'm staying with Mira."

Daddy said, "Inez," but that was all. He took my hand and we went upstairs. I fell asleep as fast as could be.

At breakfast the next morning, I found out the wake was not over. There was another whole day of it.

Three people I did not know came right after lunch. They only stayed for a few minutes, but then Mrs. Tait and another lady came. They were the first ones to sit down.

Mrs. Tait is the only person I ever saw with dark skin. Mira told me one time that there are lots of places where everyone has skin that colour, but I have not been to any of those places.

The ladies talked to Mother and Daddy for a while and then they came over and sat down—one on each side of me.

"Hello, Bethany," Mrs. Tait said. "It's been a while since I've seen you—do you remember me?"

I nodded. "Mrs. Tait," I said.

"That's right, honey. Now, I don't know if you ever met Mrs. Fleming before. Did you?"

I shook my head.

Mrs. Fleming took hold of my hand. "I'm sorry to be meeting you at such a sad time," she said. "And I'm so very sorry about your sister."

"Thank you," I said.

"I've been praying for your family," Mrs. Tait said, taking my other hand. "Started when Mira took ill, and now that the Good Lord has seen fit to take her home, I'm lifting up the rest of you every chance I get."

"Okay," I said. "Thank you." I did not know exactly what she meant but it sounded nice.

They stayed for a while and whenever no one else was at the wake, Mother and Daddy sat down and talked with them. Mrs. Tait asked if she could say a prayer before they left and we all held hands in a circle.

After they were gone, Mother kept saying to Daddy,

"Of all people," and "They didn't even mind holding our hands."

Daddy said everyone else would come around too. He said to just give them time.

Part Three

In areas where rain is not plentiful, a rain shadow may contribute to arid conditions for many miles beyond the mountains. For example, the Gobi Desert lies in the rain shadow of the Himalayas while the Atacama Desert lies in the rain shadow of the Andes.

Chapter Ten

I finally went back to school. Mother kept me home for a week after the funeral. She said it would look disrespectful to Mira if I went to class the very next day like nothing had happened.

The only place Mother let me go was to Mrs. Goldsborough's house, and that was only once. I had a strange feeling when I went across the field between our houses and knocked on her door. It made me think about the last time I was there, and how Mrs. Goldsborough looked laying in the hall, at the bottom of the stairs, like a broken doll.

Miss Kerr, the lady who was taking care of her, let me in and I saw that Mrs. Goldsborough was sitting in her favourite chair. The big white cast was still on her leg and it was up on a stool. When she saw me she held her arms out.

"Come on over here—just mind my bad leg."

I leaned on the other side of her where there was no cast and she pulled me right onto the chair beside her.

"My dear child, I've been thinking about you day and night," she said. She snuggled me against her and kissed the top of my head.

"I wanted to come and see you before, but the quarantine happened and I had to wait," I told her.

"Don't you worry about that. Now, tell me how you are. I've spoken with your mother on the telephone a few times but, of course, she hasn't felt much like talking."

"I am sad a lot," I said. "Because my sister died."

Mrs. Goldsborough did not say anything but she hugged me tight against her. When she did that, it seemed like something burst inside me. I started to cry really hard. I cried and cried and cried. Mrs. Goldsborough did not tell me everything was okay or hush me. She cried too and after a while, when I stopped, she reached in her sweater pocket and got out one Kleenex for me and one for her.

We wiped our faces and blew our noses. Then Miss Kerr came into the room and said that Mother had called and I should go home now.

That was the only time I got to leave the house the whole week after Mira's funeral. It was even worse than the quarantine, because when we had the quarantine I could still play outside. After Mira died I had to stay in the house because Mother said it would not look right for me to be romping around the yard.

I do not know if a house has feelings, but our house seemed like it was sad, just like Mother and Daddy and me.

The morning I went back to school Mr. Wolnoth put my coat on the hook for me. He said he was there to help with anything else I needed. He said all I had to do was ask. I said, "Thank you," even though I had not needed any help with my coat—I put it on the hook by myself all the time.

Before we started our lessons, Mr. Wolnoth told the class that he wanted everyone's careful attention.

"Bethany Anderson is back today for the first time since her family's tragedy. I want all of you to be especially kind to Bethany in the coming days and weeks."

At recess, a lot of kids told me they were sad that my sister died and they hoped I would feel better soon and things like that. Lawrence Philpot said he was sorry about Mira and then he said I could have half of his orange if I wanted.

Sharon Goldrick came over. She stood beside me with her head down. After a few minutes she said, "I guess everyone has forgotten that *I* was Mira's best friend."

Sharon said that her heart was breaking and she would never forget Mira—not in a million years. Some of the girls gathered around and hugged her.

"I will never, ever, *ever* have another friend like Mira," Sharon said. Then she cried and some of the others cried too and a few of them said they had been close to Mira too—even if it was not as close as Sharon—and they would miss Mira forever.

My friend Lizzie made a sour face. She whispered, "Sharon isn't happy unless she's the centre of attention."

"But she really *was* Mira's best friend," I said.

Lizzie rolled her eyes. "That's no reason for her to go on the way she does. She's been chumming for weeks with Joan Corbett and Edith Wawrykow, and she seemed as happy as a lark if you ask me."

Lizzie knows more than I do about most things because she is not slow like me. But that did not mean she knew more about everything, like when your sister dies. Lizzie only has brothers and anyway none of them ever died.

I did not like what Lizzie said about Sharon. Maybe Sharon was very sad inside. You cannot always tell what somebody is feeling just by looking at them.

For a few days everyone was nice to me like Mr. Wolnoth wanted. After that things went back to normal. I liked normal the best and I liked being at school. It was better to be at school than at home when Daddy was not there.

Especially because it seemed like something was wrong with Mother.

Chapter Eleven

Mother sat in Mira's room a lot. Sometimes she held Mira's pillow on her face and rocked back and forth. Other times she looked at pictures Mira drew before she died, or turned the pages in the notebooks of Mira's schoolwork. Turn, turn, turn. Her hand moved very slow and her head went back and forth looking at the pages.

But lots of times she just sat there, not looking at anything or holding anything or moving at all.

Daddy said Mother was saying goodbye to Mira in her own way, and I should not bother her when she was in there. I tried to obey, but if there was a phone call or a visitor for Mother, I had to go and get her. When I did that she looked at me strange, like she did not understand what I just said.

Other times Mother was angry at me, only I did not always know what I did wrong.

One morning, Miss Kerr came to our back door with a loaf of banana bread.

"Mrs. Goldsborough is getting around a good deal better now," she told Mother. "She sent this over to let you know she's thinking of you."

"Tell her thank you," Mother said. She took the banana bread.

"She asked me to let you know, as well, that Bethany is very welcome to come over if you can spare her this weekend. She's no trouble whatsoever."

After she said that, Miss Kerr looked past Mother into the kitchen and smiled at me.

I smiled back at her. "Can you spare me this weekend, Mother?" I asked.

"We'll see," Mother said. She stepped back from the doorway and started to close the door even though Miss Kerr had not said she had to be going.

"Thank you, again," Mother said, and shut the door all the way.

I could see Miss Kerr crossing our yard on her way back to Mrs. Goldsborough's house from our kitchen window. She was holding her head up like she was practising walking with a book on her head. My Aunt Tina showed me and Mira how to do that one time. She said it would help us have good posture, only I do not actually know how a book can do that.

Miss Kerr was going through the field between our

house and Mrs. Goldsborough's house when Mother came and stood close beside me.

"How dare you," she said.

"What did I do, Mother?" I said. My tummy got shaky and scared when Mother was angry and I did not know why.

"As if you didn't know," Mother said. "Don't you *ever* put me on the spot like that again."

I tried to say, "What spot, Mother?" but nothing came out. After a few minutes, Mother sat at the table and put her head down and started to cry. I went very quiet up the stairs and stayed in my room until Daddy came home from work.

When the weekend came I did not ask if I could go to Mrs. Goldsborough's house. Anyway, I did not mind too much because Daddy was home then and Mother did not spend so much time in Mira's room.

On Saturday, we went to the grocery store. I liked shopping there. I liked the smells in different parts of the store, except where the dog food is.

When we got inside, I forgot for one tiny minute that my sister died and I asked Mother, "Is it my turn to push the cart?"

Mother stopped moving. She turned her head and stared at me.

"Yes, Bethany. It is your turn. It will always be *your* turn. Are you happy now?"

Tears came in my eyes. Not because of what Mother said, but because I remembered about Mira. She was never having a turn at pushing the cart again.

"It was an innocent mistake," Daddy said.

"I'm sorry, Mother," I whispered.

All of a sudden Mother's face went sad and crumply. She squatted down in front of me and wiped the tears off my cheeks with her fingers. She hugged me and kissed my nose. "You don't need to be sorry, sweetheart," she said. "I'm the one who should be sorry. You didn't do anything wrong."

But I *did* do wrong things lots of other days. Mostly, I did not know they were wrong until after I did them. That made me wish I knew how to write more words. Then I could have made a list of things I should not do so I would not forget them and keep upsetting Mother. At bedtime, I said the ones I could remember over and over in my head.

Rules change when your sister dies. You cannot do some of the things you used to do. You cannot stomp on the stairs or clomp up and down the hall. But you cannot be too quiet either because then you sneak up on people and scare them half to death. You have to learn how to walk just right.

You cannot scrape your fork on your plate, or lean one shoe on top of the other when you take them off, or tap your fingers on the table, or leave the bathroom light on. There are a lot of other things too—and that is why it was hard for me to remember all of them.

Sometimes, even when I did not forget any of the new

rules, Mother still got angry with me. One day, I found out why.

I was putting bowls on the table for lunch. All of a sudden Mother smacked her hand on the kitchen counter and said, very loud, "Why did you answer the door that day? *Why*?"

I did not know what day she meant. But after a minute she said, "If you hadn't let those awful people into the house, your sister would still be alive. You know that, don't you?"

Then I understood that she meant the people who were passing through on their way north. A terrible squeezing feeling came into me and it was hard to get a breath. I could not make myself look at Mother and I did not want to see her eyes. It felt like we were standing there for a long time.

When I could make my voice work again, I said, "Is it my fault Mira died?"

"You figure it out," Mother said. Then she turned off the burner for the soup she was making and went upstairs to her room.

That was when I understood why Mother kept getting so angry with me.

But that was not the whole reason.

Chapter Twelve

After a few days, Mother told me she had something she needed to say to me.

"Come sit with me," she said. When I did, she put her arm around me and kissed my eyebrow.

"I am sorry for what I said to you the other day, Bethany," she said. "It was not your fault that Mira died."

But her voice did not sound like she meant it, so I did not know what was true. That made me feel like something black and scary was inside me. I wanted to ask Daddy but I was afraid to. What if Daddy did not know I was the one who let the strangers into the house that day? If I told him about it, maybe he would be angry with me too.

I tried not to look into Mira's bedroom when I walked by, but that did not really help. I still thought about her and about what Mother said in the kitchen. I wished I could go back to the day when the people stopped here on their way up north and knocked on our door. If I could do that, I would only open the door a tiny crack and I would say something to make the man get back in his car and drive away.

I would never have let that man in if I knew what would happen to Mira. I wished I could tell that to Mother but when I tried to practice it in my head, I could not figure out the right words.

"Why did they have to come here?" Mother asked Daddy one day. "Of all the houses in Manitoba, why did they come to ours?"

"There's no answer to that," Daddy said. "It's no good dwelling on something you can't change."

Then Mother went to the phone and asked the person who is called Directory Assistance for the phone number of those people. She wrote it down on a piece of paper but when she started to dial it, Daddy took the phone out of her hand and hung it up.

"What good would that do?" he asked.

Mother did not answer. She sat down on her knees on the floor beside him and held onto his legs and cried. When she saw me watching, she waved for me to go to her.

"You miss your sister, don't you, Bethany?" she said.

"Yes."

"We were lucky to have her," Mother said. Then she put her head down and cried some more.

A lot of days it felt like we were going to be sad forever.

That was why I started to love to go to school. Nobody was sad there. It was all right to talk and smile and even laugh. At recess and lunch time, I went outside with Lizzie and Mary. The air smelled good and I loved playing with my friends.

Even class time did not seem so bad anymore. Mr. Wolnoth made a contest for bests and that was fun. I did not think I would ever win because I am not best at any of our subjects, but one morning Mr. Wolnoth called my name to come to the front of the room.

"Bethany Anderson is the winner of the Best Effort Certificate," Mr. Wolnoth said. "She works very hard and she never gives up."

Everyone clapped and Mr. Wolnoth gave me a rolled up paper with a ribbon tied around it, just like the others got when they won a best.

Lawrence Philpot told me, "Nice going," at lunchtime.

Another day Sandra Yarmie said she had big news to tell. Mr. Wolnoth let her make a special announcement after we said The Lord's Prayer and sang *O Canada*.

"My oldest sister and her husband had a baby boy yesterday," she said. "That makes me an aunt!"

Some of the other children clapped their hands and said "ooh" about Sandra's nephew but I did not think a new baby was very interesting. Lots of people have babies. They do not do much except eat and sleep and cry.

But then Sandra said another thing.

"They are naming the baby Wayne, after my uncle

who died in the war."

After that Meg Gainer said that when she got married and had a son she would name him after *her* uncle who died in the war. Then Violet Kaufman said she was naming her first daughter after her grandmother because it was a family tradition and some other girls talked about who they would name their babies after.

That was when I had an idea. I put my hand up to have a turn to talk.

"Yes, Bethany?" Mr. Wolnoth said. His face was surprised because I do not put my hand up in class too many times.

I stood up like we are supposed to do when we are talking to the whole school.

"When I get married, I will have a baby girl and I will name her Mira after my sister who died from polio."

I felt proud. Then I sat down again because I was finished my turn.

"Who is going to marry *you*, Bethany?" asked Jeannie Nanton.

I did not know the answer to that so I did not say anything. A few people laughed a little bit. Probably they thought Jeannie's question was silly. Nobody knows who they are going to marry when they are only twelve.

Then Mary Haig said, "Someone very lucky, that's for sure."

I looked at her. She was standing up, even though Mr. Wolnoth had not pointed to her for a turn.

Lizzie Newmarch stood up too. "That's right," she said.

"Because Bethany is always kind, and *nice*," Mary said.

"True," said Luke Haliwell. "And that's more than I can say for some people."

Mr. Wolnoth smiled and said Mary and Lizzie and Luke were absolutely right and that kindness was one of the qualities that really matters. Then he told Jeannie to stay in at recess because he would like to have a word with her.

Recess was also when Luke came over to talk to me.

"That was nice, what you said in class," he told me. "I bet you miss your sister a lot."

I did not know why, but when he said that, it made my throat hurt and tears started to come down my face. I wiped them off with my sleeve.

"I know the sadness is there all the time, in behind everything," Luke said, very soft. "But it won't always be this bad."

I was surprised when he said that. I did not think anyone knew about the sad feeling that never went away. I asked him, "Did you have a sister who died?"

Luke shook his head. "But I did lose somebody," he said.

Then he did not say anything else and I did not say anything else. But he stayed standing with me until Mr. Wolnoth rang the bell for class to start again.

Chapter Thirteen

Christmas was coming. Only, it did not feel like it at our house because we were sad and Mira was not there. Mira and I used to help Mother bake gingerbread men and Christmas cakes and decorate the house. Mira loved to spray pretend snow on the windows and put the manger scene on the coffee table. Sometimes we cut snowflakes out of paper and tied strings to them for Daddy to hang from the doorway and we made long strings of popcorn for the tree.

The Christmas after Mira died Daddy brought home a tree and put it in the corner of the living room in the red stand with white snowflakes painted on it.

The first day it was there he asked Mother, "Do you want me to get the decorations out of the attic?"

"Not today," Mother said. "Wait until I feel up to it."

After a few days, Daddy got the boxes anyway. He told Mother he would go ahead and put the lights on the tree so it would be ready whenever she was. Mother told him to suit himself.

I helped Daddy test the light bulbs. We had to change two blue ones and a green one on one of the strings. Then he put them on the tree and plugged it in. It looked pretty even without the ornaments and tinsel and candy canes and popcorn strings.

When I got home from school the next day, I ran in to see it. Mother was sitting on the couch, looking at it.

"Hello, Mother," I said.

Mother made a sound which was not a word but means "hello" anyway.

"Do you feel like decorating the tree today, Mother?" I asked.

I did not think Mother would say "yes," but maybe she would tell me, "You go ahead and do it, Bethany," and then I would put things on the tree up as high as I could reach.

Only, Mother did not tell me that. She looked at me and then she stared at the tree. After a minute, she got up and walked over and stood in front of it.

"We're just going to act like Mira never existed, is that it?" she said. "We're going to carry on like she was nothing to us?"

I wanted to run up the stairs to my room but I was afraid that would make Mother angrier.

"I'm sorry, Mother," I said.

"I'm *sorry*, Mother. I'm *sorry*, Mother," Mother said.

All of a sudden, Mother leaned forward and grabbed the tree. She gave it a big tug and it fell over. Water ran out of the red stand with white snowflakes painted on it. Mother pulled the tree across the floor.

"I'm not having it," Mother said. She was breathing funny and her face had red blotches on it. "This is my house."

Then the tree stopped moving and Mother jerked back a little bit. The reason of that was because the lights were plugged in. Mother gave a bigger yank and the plug came out. Mother pulled the tree out of the living room and down the hall and that is when I got behind the chair in the corner and squeezed myself as small as I could.

I heard the back door but I did not move. There was a ka-thunk, ka-thunk sound in my ears, which was from my heart feeling scared. Then I heard the door open again.

Mother came back. I could hear her standing in the doorway of the living room. She was taking big breaths like she had been running. I tried to be quiet so she would not come and look down over the top of the chair. It felt like my heart might burst if that happened.

Only, Mother did not come over to the corner where I was hiding. She went to the boxes of decorations and I could tell from the scuffing sounds that she was pushing them across the floor. They scraped down the hall and I heard the door again.

table. He looked over at Mrs. Goldsborough and Miss Kerr.

"I want to thank you ladies for taking care of Bethany," he said.

"That's what neighbours are for," Mrs. Goldsborough said. "And I hope you know you needn't worry about a word of this going anywhere else."

"Thank you," Daddy said. "Inez has been struggling."

"It's a terrible heartache, to lose a child," Mrs. Goldsborough said.

After I had my dessert, Daddy said it was time to go. I said, "Thank you for supper," because that is good manners. I was surprised to see our car in Mrs. Goldsborough's driveway when I went outside with Daddy.

Daddy opened the door for me and I got in. Something felt wrong. I looked in the back and there was a suitcase on the seat.

Daddy got in too. He turned sideways and said, "Mommy needs to rest for a while, honey."

I did not say anything.

"While Mommy is getting better, you're going to stay with Aunt Edith and Uncle Harold."

"I do not want to," I said.

"I'm afraid you have to," Daddy said. "Mommy isn't well enough to take care of you right now."

I did not talk to Daddy the whole drive to my Aunt Edith and Uncle Harold's house. When he said things like, "You'll be able to play with your cousins," and

"Won't that be fun?" I looked out the window and did not answer.

I have three cousins. Kenny and Rose and Carl. I do not like them very much. They are nice to me sometimes but other times they act like I am not even there. If I talk, they ask each other, "Do you hear a strange noise in here?"

One time last summer Kenny called me the thing I do not like. Then Mira twisted his arm behind his back and made him say he was sorry and he would never do it again. I am not sure why Mira did that when she called me that herself sometimes.

When we got to Aunt Edith and Uncle Harold's house, Daddy said, "Bethany, none of this is easy for any of us. Please don't give me a hard time."

He got out of the car and took the suitcase to the door. I made my feet scrape on the ground when I went behind him but I do not think he cared.

Daddy opened the door and called, "We're here!"

Aunt Edith came down the hall and told Daddy to put my things in Rose's room.

"The girls will be company for each other," Aunt Edith said.

Daddy patted my suitcase and said he hoped everything I needed was in there. He came and hugged me but I kept my arms straight down and did not hug him back.

"It will only be for a few days," he said.

"How many is a few?" I said, even though I did not

want to talk to Daddy.

"It won't be long, honey," Daddy said. "We want you home as soon as possible."

But soon did not happen very fast.

Chapter Fifteen

My cousins were nice the first day. They played tiddlywinks with me and never called me a name, not even once. When it was bedtime, Rose told me, "Sweet dreams."

In the morning Aunt Edith asked me how I entertain myself at home. She said I should find things to keep myself busy and not expect my cousins to spend all of their time with me.

At bedtime Rose told me not to squirm so much when I am sleeping. I do not know how to stop from doing something when I am asleep so I tried to stay awake. That did not work.

The next morning Rose told Aunt Edith that I kicked all night. She said, "I don't see why I have to be the one stuck with her."

Aunt Edith said she would see what she could figure out. That night she told me I would sleep in the
study. Uncle Harold brought a camping mattress from
the basement and blew it up. Aunt Edith put a blanket
on it.

I did not like sleeping in the study when my aunt and
uncle and cousins were all in the bedrooms upstairs.
The downstairs felt big and dark. There were scary
sounds and even though I told myself they were just
house noises like Daddy always says, I was not so sure.
Also, the mattress smelled like a bicycle tire and when I
turned over I kept rolling off it.

I wished I was home in my own bed.

I wished my sister had not died.

Nothing has been right since that happened.

Daddy came to see me every day. The first day, before
he got there, Aunt Edith asked me did I want to help
Daddy or did I want to make things harder for him.

"Help," I said.

"If you really want to help, don't pester your father
about going home. And when he asks how you like it
here, you tell him you like it just fine."

I did *not* like it there fine. I did not like it *one bit* but I
did not say that because that would be rude.

"But I *do* want to go home," I said.

"Maybe so, but saying that to your father will only

make him feel bad and it won't get you home any sooner. The man has enough to deal with at the moment without worrying about you. So, no long face, you hear me?"

I did my best, even though I am not good at that kind of pretend. Every day when Daddy asked me how I was doing and I told him fine I thought Daddy would know I was not telling the truth. But he just said he was glad to hear it.

On Christmas day Mother came with Daddy. They brought presents. I got a jigsaw puzzle and a new sweater and scarf that matched. I said "thank you", but I did not care about the presents. I only wanted to go home.

Later, we all had turkey dinner. Aunt Edith told Mother three times that she was not eating enough to keep a bird alive. After the last time, Mother said, "You bury a child and see how hungry you are."

No one said anything for a while after that.

When Aunt Edith went to the kitchen to get tea and plum pudding, Mother told Daddy she wanted to go home. Daddy went to tell Aunt Edith and then he and Mother said goodbye to everybody.

I could not eat my plum pudding. Aunt Edith said she would cover it and I could have it later when I felt like it.

It was the terriblest Christmas ever.

🌢

More days went by. Daddy kept bringing things for me

from home. He brought my doll named Belinda who closes her eyes when she lies down, and some of my toys and my colouring things. One day he brought *Make Way for Ducklings.* That made me a little bit happy because I did not think he had noticed me practising my reading.

But mostly I felt sad. It seemed like pretty soon all of my things would be at my aunt and uncle's house and maybe if that happened I would stay there forever.

Sometimes Aunt Edith made Rose and Kenny and Carl play with me. One day they said we were going to have a game of hide and seek. That is a very fun game but they did not play it right.

Kenny was It. When he started to count, I went and hid in the closet by the front door where everybody hangs their coats. I waited and waited but Kenny did not find me.

A closet is not a hard hiding place to find. Not like on top of a wardrobe or in a secret cubbyhole. That is how I knew they tricked me. Maybe they were waiting to see how long it would be before I came out. Or maybe they were hoping I would keep waiting and waiting, and they would not have to play with me.

After a while I heard my cousins laughing and talking quiet.

I did not want to cry only I could not help it. I pushed myself back into the corner of the closet as far as I could go. I tried to be quiet but Rose heard me. She came and pulled the closet door open.

"Shush your crying, now, Bethany," she said. "It was just a joke."

I did not answer. My throat hurt.

"Stop that sniffling before Mother hears you," Rose said. "Come out and we'll play a real game this time."

I stopped crying but I did not move. Rose made herself smile.

"That's a good girl," she said. "Come on now."

I shook my head. That made Rose angry. She told me to stop being a baby and come out this minute. I did not move. Then she reached in and grabbed my arm and tried to pull me out. So I bit her hand.

Rose yelled a little bit and Kenny came to see why.

"The halfwit bit me," she whispered to him. "Can you believe that?"

"Leave her in there if that's how she's going to act," Kenny said.

And they did, which suited me just fine. I found out that I *liked* being in the closet. No one bothered me or made fun of me. No one tried to trick me to walk on a rug so they could pull it and make me fall. That could make anybody fall, but if you have one leg shorter than the other, it will happen for sure.

The closet was quiet and nice. I started to go there when I wanted to be by myself. After a few days I had the idea to go in there at night too. It was better than sleeping on the stinky camping mattress. I took the blanket and wrapped it around me, curled up in the corner and went to sleep. I felt warm and safe and happy. The sounds the house made did not bother me when I was in there.

In the morning, I snuck back to the study as soon as I heard my aunt and uncle start to move around upstairs. Except the third morning. I did not hear anything until Aunt Edith screeched that I was gone. That is how I got caught.

Aunt Edith did not like it one bit.

"Why on earth would you do such an odd thing?" she said. "Your father is going to hear about this—don't think he isn't."

There was a lot of whispering in the house that day. Kenny and Carl and Rose whispered to each other and also to Aunt Edith. Aunt Edith whispered to Uncle Harold when he got home after work.

There was no whispering to Daddy when he came to see me. Aunt Edith sent me upstairs to Rose's room so she could talk to him in private. Only, it was not really private because Uncle Harold and Rose were there too.

I went upstairs but I did not go to Rose's room. I went to a secret place Carl and Kenny showed me one day before Christmas, where they could listen to things people were saying downstairs. They said it was a good way to find out things they were not supposed to know, like what presents they were getting for Christmas.

I put my face down on the metal grate in the place they showed me and listened to what Aunt Edith was saying to Daddy.

The first thing she said was that I slept in the closet.

Then she said she was not telling him his business, but in her opinion I needed to see a head doctor. She said she cannot tolerate the way I sit and stare at nothing, or the peculiar things I say and do. After that, she told Rose to go ahead and tell him what I did to her.

Rose told Daddy that I bit her for no reason and now she was afraid to be around me. And Uncle Harold said they did not want to add to Daddy's problems, but they were at the end of their rope. He said it was not fair to their own children, to have to worry about being bitten and so forth.

Daddy did not say anything all the time Aunt Edith and Rose and Uncle Harold were talking. After they were finished he said he was sorry they had been in-convenienced and he appreciated all they had done. He told Rose to please call me to come downstairs.

I was a little bit scared going down the stairs, until I saw Daddy's face. He opened his arms up and I ran into them and he hugged me very hard. Then he said, "Let's gather up your things, sweetheart. It's time to go."

Chapter Sixteen

On the drive home Daddy told me, "We have to give your mom time." I did not ask time for what. I was too happy and excited to be going back to my own home. I could not stop bouncing in my seat and clapping my hands.

When we went inside, Mother looked at me and then at Daddy and said, "What's going on?"

"I'll explain everything later," Daddy said. "But I'll tell you one thing. This little lady is sure glad to be back."

After that Daddy took my suitcase upstairs and helped me put everything away. He said, "You'll be back to school next week. In the meantime, try not to ask too much of your mother—wait until I'm home and I'll take care of whatever you need."

I did my best. It was not that hard because Mother

spent a lot of time in Mira's room or sitting in the living room staring at the wall. The first day, when it was time for lunch, she forgot to make anything. I asked did she want me to make us peanut butter and jam sandwiches.

"You go ahead," Mother said. "I might have something later on."

Mostly, I played in my room or outside if it was not too cold. I tried not to bother Mother because Daddy said and also because the way she looked at me sometimes made my stomach feel funny.

People came to visit but Mother did not feel up to company. I liked it when they brought food because Mother also did not feel up to cooking most days and Daddy did not know how to make many things. He mostly opened canned beans or made scrambled eggs.

Mrs. Tait brought a big jar of cabbage soup and some biscuits. Mrs. Haliwell came with chicken pot pie and Mr. Oleson dropped off fresh rolls and cold pork roast that his wife sent.

The day before school started again, Mrs. Melchyn came over with a pan of lasagna and a cinnamon loaf. She told Daddy she was leaving that week to spend the rest of the winter with her sister in Sarnia. Before she left, she hugged me and said quiet in my ear that she prays for me every day.

I hugged her back very hard and I made a memory in my head to say God Bless Mrs. Melchyn in my bedtime prayers.

I was really and truly glad to go back to school. I did not even mind if it was freezing waiting for the bus in the morning.

Lizzie and Mary were happy to see me. We all said we had missed each other but we had not missed school. Only, I did not mean the part about school. Then they told me about their Christmas presents and I told them about mine.

After that Mary told us her grandma and grandpa came to visit on the holidays and her grandpa showed her how to do a trick with string. It was like magic. I said I would like to know how to do a trick like that.

Mary tried to teach me how to do it at recess but she gave up after a while. She said it would be easier when the weather was warm again and we could sit on the grass. Also, we had to watch out for boys and snowballs and that made it very hard to pay attention.

On our very first day back in school, Mr. Wolnoth gave us a pop spelling quiz. That is a surprise test but it is not a good kind of surprise. Lizzie got a Best Spelling Certificate for getting all corrects on it and Mary said Lizzie will win a bee someday. That is not a kind of bee that makes honey and stings you. It is a big room where you do spelling out loud in front of judges. There is a prize for the winner, so I hope Mary is right that Lizzie will win it.

And then, the second week back to school, the wonderfulest thing happened. I read *Make Way for Ducklings* all by myself. I had to start over three times but I finally did it. It was hard but I had been practicing every day because I am the girl at school who is the best at effort. Mr. Wolnoth was very proud of me. He said that just goes to show what happens when you keep trying. Then he told everybody to give me a big hand, which means to clap for me, and they did.

I think that was my best day at school so far, except for one thing. I was sad that Mira did not get to hear me read her favourite book from when she was little. It is very hard when your sister dies and you never get to see her or tell her anything again.

At recess that day, Lizzie hugged me because I read *Make Way for Ducklings* and she told me soon I will even be able to read books for the bigger grades. I am not too excited about that because some of those books have no pictures.

I was liking school more and more. Way more than I ever thought I would. Also, I wished we could stay in class until it was time for Daddy to come home. I did not like to be there when it was only me and Mother.

One day when I got home from school, Mother was sitting bent over on Mira's bed, rocking back and forth, holding a pillow that had Mira's sweater wrapped around it. When I went by I heard her say something, so I stopped and went back.

"Did you want something, Mother?" I asked.

Mother's head lifted up very slow. Her face did not look right and her voice sounded strange and low.

"Get...out...of...my...sight."

I walked fast to my room and closed the door. I sat on the bed and took big, slow breaths like Daddy said I should if I ever felt scared. Then I started to worry that Mother might come to my room.

My own mother coming into my room should not be scary at all.

I tried to tell myself that. I whispered, "I do not have to be afraid of Mother."

I said it over and over. Only, I did not think I was saying the truth.

I thought about tiptoeing out of my room and walking as quiet as a mouse down the hall past Mira's room. Probably Mother was leaning over the pillow again. I might be able to go by the doorway without her seeing me.

I went to my door and touched the knob, but when I tried to make myself turn it and go out, my knees felt trembly. So I sat back down on my bed and listened to see if Mother might be coming.

I waited and listened for a long time until I heard the wonderful sound of Daddy's car. Then Daddy was in the kitchen downstairs calling, "Where are my girls?"

After that it was easy to open the door and run past Mira's room and down the stairs. I grabbed Daddy and started to cry.

Daddy asked and asked what was wrong.

Mother came into the kitchen. She said, "She misses her sister, what do you think?"

"Is that it?" Daddy said. And I nodded because I could not say the truth with Mother standing there.

At home, Mother got quieter and quieter. She did not talk to me or Daddy hardly at all. Mostly, she only said yes or no if we asked her a question. Whenever she went into Mira's room, she closed the door and did not want to be disturbed. Lots of days when I got home from school, she was already there.

Then another bad day happened.

I was in the living room, behind the chair in the corner of the room. There is a window beside that chair and I was looking out at the snow falling. I love the way snowflakes float down so soft and beautiful.

After a while the snow made me tired. I fell asleep. That was why I did not see Daddy come home. I did not hear him come in the door or call for his girls so I did not run to meet him like the other days.

The thing I *did* hear was a loud bang. I woke up and opened my eyes and blinked until I remembered why I was behind the chair. When I started to move, the foot on my short leg was prickly from being laid on so I stuck my leg out and wiggled my toes. That was why I did not stand up and go out to the kitchen, and that was how I heard what Mother said to Daddy.

"I can't do it, Jack. I can't stand it anymore."

Daddy said, "We're all hurting."

"Don't act like you don't know what I mean," Mother said.

Daddy said, "Watch what you say."

"You don't know how I feel, watching her hobble around the house with that blank face and open mouth."

"Stop!" Daddy said. He said it loud but Mother kept talking.

"Then tell me why! *Why, Jack*? If we had to lose a child, why did it have to be Mira? My beautiful, perfect girl. Why *her*?"

I stopped wiggling my toes.

It was cold by the window but I did not move.

There was a strange sound from the kitchen and then Mother screamed, "Don't you touch me. Don't you dare touch me!"

After that there were terrible noises. Glass breaking and something scraping on the floor. Bumps and thuds. I put my head down and covered my ears with my hands but I could not keep the sounds out.

Other things happened that night.

Doctor Mynarski came. He told Daddy that he was giving Mother something to calm her. When he left, Mother went with him. He helped her walk to the car and get in.

Daddy found me hiding behind the chair. He asked me what I had heard. I said I heard dishes breaking.

Daddy told me that people do things they would not normally do when they are crazy with grief. He said

Mother had gone away to a rest home to get better and that when she comes back everything will be fine.

It was harder and harder to believe the things he told me.

Part Four

It is a mistake to assume that nothing can grow in a rain shadow. In fact, drought resistant plant life often exists in these areas. While the land in a rain shadow may not be lush and green like the windward side of a mountain, there will typically be a few trees, shrubs, or flowers growing bravely and keeping each other company, even in difficult conditions.

Chapter Seventeen

A secret is something you do not want other people to know. Like if you did something wrong, or took something that was not yours, which I did the time I took the half penny that belonged to Gracie.

The problem is that it is hard to keep a secret. Even a secret about yourself that you do not want anyone to find out. The reason of that is that you feel better after you tell it.

We used to have a cat named Maxwell. I told him all the things I did not want to tell to anyone else. It made me feel better even though Maxwell did not understand what I was saying to him. But one day Maxwell started to make Mira sneeze, so he had to go and live with another family. I do not know who.

I had not told *anyone* my new secrets. Not Mrs.

Goldsborough or Mary Haig or Lizzie Newmarch. Not even Daddy.

He did not know that ever since I came back from staying at Aunt Edith and Uncle Harold's house I was frightened of Mother. When I thought about her coming back from the rest home, my mouth got dry and my stomach hurt.

I could not tell that to anyone.

Daddy also did not know that Mira died because of me. I did not know what would happen if he found out that I let the people who made her sick into the house.

And Daddy knew what Mother said to him the day she went away but he did not know I heard it.

That was the thing I could not stop thinking about.

When Mother said, "If we had to lose a child, why did it have to be *Mira*?" I tried to trick myself that I did not really understand it. Only, I did.

Mother wished that it was me who died instead of Mira. Mother could not stand looking at me and thinking about what I am like and remembering that her perfect daughter is dead and I am still here.

One day, after Mother went away, I went into Mira's room and sat on the bed. I tried to imagine how it would feel to be like her. If I could be smart and pretty and walk right, Mother might not wish I had died.

But I know that cannot happen. I can never be the beautiful, perfect child. I can only be me—Bethany. The girl who limps and can only read one book.

That is why I think Daddy is wrong when he says everything will be better when Mother comes home.

While Mother was at the rest home, I went to Mrs. Goldsborough's house after school. Miss Kerr was not there every day because Mrs. Goldsborough's leg was not broken anymore. Miss Kerr came two times a week and did things in the house that Mrs. Goldsborough was getting too old to do. Also, she helped Mrs. Goldsborough take a bath and wash her hair.

I stayed there until Daddy was finished work and came to take me home for supper. Daddy was learning to cook new things and I was his helper. We made pork chops with boiled potatoes, spaghetti, and cheeseburgers. Sometimes our cooking was not that good but we always said it was delicious to each other.

Daddy had been helping me with a special project for school. It was a big assignment that Mr. Wolnoth gave to all the grades.

The special project was about weather and we were planning a big Weather Fair for when everyone was finished. I never saw that kind of fair before but Mr. Wolnoth said all of the projects would be on display and everyone in Junction would be invited.

I did not know if everyone would come. Probably all the mothers and fathers would come and also some aunts and uncles and grandparents. That is who mostly comes to our music recitals at the end of the school year. But the music recitals are not very good. Maybe the Weather Fair would be better.

The project Mr. Wolnoth gave to me was called,

"Snow". I had to make a model of snow and tell three things about it. I finished the second part very quick. I told Daddy the things I wanted to tell about snow and he helped me write them down on a paper. This was what it said:

Snow

by Bethany Anderson

1.) Snow is cold.

2.) Snow is white.

3.) Snow falls out of the sky.

Daddy said those were very good things to tell about snow.

He helped me work on the model too. It was not the kind of model which is a lady who wears clothes and stands funny. My model was an empty shoebox with pretend snow. There was snow falling into the box and snow inside the box.

The snow falling into the box was tiny snowflakes I cut out from paper. That was the slow part to make. Daddy was hanging them from threads which were stuck to plastic you can see through. Daddy made a frame for it so the snowflakes could hang down.

The snow inside the box was made from Kleenexes which I tore into tiny, tiny pieces. It looked very real.

I was hoping for a good mark on my project about snow because it was a lot of work and I did my best.

Mary Haig's project was called, "Thunderstorms". She

said it would have sound effects, which would be very thrilling. Everybody in the whole school had a different weather. I never knew before that there were so many kinds.

Mira's friend Sharon Goldrick thought Mr. Wolnoth's wife was behind the whole idea. She said Mr. Wolnoth never made anyone do projects before he went and got married.

I did not know if that was true. If it was, I was glad Mr. Wolnoth got married. I was excited for the Weather Fair.

Chapter Eighteen

On the weekend, we went to the rest place to visit Mother. It looked exactly like a house, only bigger. I was surprised when we went inside because Mother and all the other people were sitting in chairs in a big room. I think they would be able to rest better in beds.

Daddy said we were glad to see Mother and Mother said she was glad to see us, too. She did not say much after that. Daddy talked a lot. He told her everything about Mrs. Goldsborough and about the things we can cook now. When he finished telling her about those things, Daddy said maybe Mother would like to hear all about my snow project. I told her how I made the snowflakes for hanging and for inside the box. And I told her about the Weather Fair we were going to have when everybody finished making their projects.

"Wouldn't it be nice if Mommy was home in time to go to the Weather Fair?" Daddy said.

"Don't put ideas in her head," Mother said.

"Okay, fine, but you must be getting anxious to get out of here yourself, aren't you?" Daddy said.

"If you're just coming here to pressure me, you might as well stay home," Mother said. She stood up. "To tell you the truth, I'm a little tired anyway. You two might as well get started on the drive back."

Daddy said, "Okay," and gave Mother a hug. She started to walk away, but she only went a few steps. Then she turned around and came back.

"You know what, Jack—there's no point to this."

Daddy's mouth opened but he closed it without saying anything.

"I can't go back there and live in that house and act as if this is my life now and that's fine. Because it's not fine—and it never will be."

"If you just gave yourself a little more time—" Daddy said.

"No, Jack. It's not going to work," Mother said. "I *am* leaving here soon but I'm not coming back to Junction. My mind is made up."

Daddy said he didn't want to hear anymore right then and Mother said he was going to have to hear it sometime. They stood still and looked at each other for a little bit but nobody said anything else. Then Daddy said we'd be going and we got in the car and drove home.

Mrs. Goldsborough fell again. She did not fall down the stairs that time. She slipped on the mat in front of the kitchen sink and fell on the floor. Miss Kerr was there and helped her up and called the doctor.

Doctor Mynarski said there would be a bad bruise but nothing was broken. That was good news but after that he said he did not think Mrs. Goldsborough should be living by herself anymore. He said she is not steady enough on her feet.

Mrs. Goldsborough told me about it when I went there after school.

"Who will live with you?" I said. "Will it be Miss Kerr?"

"I'm afraid that isn't how it's going to work," Mrs. Goldsborough said. "I'll be going to live with my son and his wife."

"Do I know them?"

"You met them once when they were visiting, but that was a long time ago," Mrs. Goldsborough said. "You were too young to remember."

"Where do they live?"

"In a place called Morden."

"Is that close to here?"

"It's more than a hundred miles away," Mrs. Goldsborough said.

"When are you coming back?" I asked.

Mrs. Goldsborough looked very sad. "I don't suppose

I'll ever live here again."

"But this is your house," I said. It did not seem possible that Mrs. Goldsborough's house could be next door to us without Mrs. Goldsborough in it.

Mrs. Goldsborough's son was there the next day when I went after school. He told me thank you for how I helped his mother when she fell the first time, and for being a good neighbour and friend to her.

"She is a good neighbour and friend to me, too," I said. "I do not want her to move away because I will miss her."

"She will miss you too, Bethany," he said, "But she can't live alone anymore. We don't want any harm to come to her, do we?"

I did not want that so I told him, "No." Then he said I probably would not see Mrs. Goldsborough again and I should go and say my goodbyes.

It was really, really hard to tell Mrs. Goldsborough goodbye. We both cried very hard. She said she loved me and I said I loved her. It felt like my heart was broken.

I did not feel like working on my snow project that night even though I had not finished cutting out all the snowflakes. Daddy said there was plenty of time left and there was no reason I could not take the night off.

Mrs. Goldsborough's son took her away to live in Morden—not the next day but the day after that. Then a man came and put a sign up in front of her house. Daddy told me it said the house was for rent. I made a plan in my head that I would never *ever* like anyone else who lived in Mrs. Goldsborough's house.

After Mrs. Goldsborough was gone, Daddy had to get a new babysitter for me for after school. That was a girl named Thea who was in the school for older grades.

Most days Thea was nice and played Snap or Snakes and Ladders with me. And she read part of a book to me, which was called *The Hundred Dresses*. In that story there was a girl named Wanda who always wore the same dress to school and other girls teased her. Then she told them that she had a hundred dresses at home. It was a very interesting story. I do not think Wanda really had a hundred dresses at home or she would not have worn the old blue dress every day.

Thea was not so nice on days when she was in a terrible foul mood.

She would tell me when she opened the door, "Don't expect any fun and games today, Bethany. I am in a terrible foul mood."

I did not mind that very much. Even on those days Thea was never mean to me. She just did not want to be bothered. She would tell me to find something to do until my father came. And she let me look at her comics if I wanted to. Usually I did.

Chapter Nineteen

Mrs. Goldsborough had only been gone for one whole week and part of another week when somebody started moving into her house. Daddy told me about it after he picked me up from Thea's house and we went home to make supper.

"It sure rented fast," he said.

"I do not want anybody else in that house," I said. "Only Mrs. Goldsborough."

"I see," Daddy said. He was peeling potatoes, which he was getting better at doing.

"Are we having pork chops?" I asked.

"Nope. Sausages," Daddy said. "So, aren't you curious about our new neighbours?"

"No," I said. Except, after Daddy asked me that, I *did* get curious.

"Is it somebody I know?" I said.

"You met the woman once. She came to Mira's wake with Mrs. Tait."

"I forget that lady's name," I said.

"Mrs. Fleming. She and her husband have rented Mrs. Goldsborough's house. They started moving in today."

I tried to make myself feel cross, only it was hard because I remembered Mrs. Fleming was nice to me when she came to our house after Mira died. So, I mostly made myself be cross about Mr. Fleming. I decided he was probably not nice like Mrs. Fleming.

For a long time after we went to the rest home, Daddy had said that Mother would come to her senses and he was just waiting her out. One day she telephoned. At first Daddy looked happy. Then he sounded angry. At the end of talking to her, I heard him say she was making a big mistake.

After that, Daddy told me that Mother had left the rest home and had gone to live by herself in another town. She got a job cleaning rooms at a motel and rented a room in a boarding house. Daddy went there to see her there but I did not go with him. I went to Thea's house even though it was a Saturday and I usually only went there on school days. When Daddy came back he told me we might as well get used to it just being the two of us for the time being.

I could tell that Daddy was sad about Mother not coming home. Sometimes I felt sad about that too, but mostly I did not mind so much. Except for one part.

I knew it was my fault Daddy was sad. If I had not let those people into the house, Mira would still be here and everything would be the way it was before. Daddy would still have Mother and Mira. Not only me.

Everyone at school knows about Mother going away to live in another town. I thought maybe it was Rose or Kenny or Carl who told, but when I asked them they all said they would not do that. Carl said that the whole town knows and some of the kids at school probably heard it from their parents.

Anyway, no one is very interested. Not like when Mother went to the rest place and some of the kids told me, "Your mother is in the nuthouse, Bethany."

This time, nobody seems to care much. Except Thea. She started to ask me questions as soon as I got to her house after school. I was not very helpful.

The first question she asked was, "Is it true your mom isn't coming back?"

"That is what she told Daddy," I said.

"So, do you know what your dad is going to do about you? After school I mean?"

I said I did not know.

"Because, when he asked me to babysit, he said it was only going to be until your mom came home. So, what happens now?"

I said I did not know that either.

"I mean, I like watching you, but I never meant to keep doing it all year. Does he know that?"

I said I did not know.

"Well, I can't. You're a nice kid and everything but this was just supposed to be for a few weeks. It's not the way I want to spend all my free time. No offence."

That was not a question so I did not have to answer.

Then Thea said, "I hate to have to tell him, though. Do you think you could do it? Just say I'm giving my notice, because I have other things I need to do after school."

"Okay," I said.

"But not *here*. Wait 'til you get home," she said. "Soon as you get to your house, go ahead and tell him."

"Okay," I said.

"You won't forget, will you? "

"No."

When Daddy picked me up, Thea whispered in my ear, "Remember—tell him the minute you get to your house."

"I will," I said. To make sure, I did a practice in my head all the way home.

Only, what did we find standing in our driveway but Mrs. Fleming.

"Hello there," she said as we got out of the car. "I thought you'd be along about now. I guess you've heard we're your new neighbours."

"Yes—we're glad to have you next door," Daddy said.

Mrs. Fleming smiled. "Well, I might be starting off on

the wrong foot," she said. "I'm here to borrow a Phillips screwdriver if you have one. We're not finished unpacking and we can't find ours."

"Certainly," Daddy said. "Come on in."

Mrs. Fleming asked me how I was doing when Daddy went to find the screwdriver. I told her I was fine and she said she was glad to hear it.

"Here we go," Daddy said. He came back into the kitchen and passed Mrs. Fleming the screwdriver. "Can I offer you a drive home? It's a little nippy, even for a short walk."

"Thanks, but I enjoy the brisk air," Mrs. Fleming said. She turned to me. "Now, you come on over and visit anytime you like. I hear you were great friends with Mrs. Goldsborough, and Jerry and I are hoping for the same."

She looked at Daddy then. "If you ever need someone to watch Bethany, we'd be more than happy to help."

That made me remember about Thea and how I was supposed to tell Daddy as soon as we got home.

"Oh!" I said. "Daddy, Thea said to tell you she is giving her notice. Because she has other things to do after school."

Daddy's face got a little bit red. He said, "We can talk about that later, honey. We don't want Mrs. Fleming to think we're hinting."

Mrs. Fleming laughed. She said. "Don't worry. Besides, we'd *love* to have a youngster around."

That was how I started to go to back to Mrs. Goldsborough's house after school, even though

Mrs. Goldsborough was not there. It was very strange the first time.

Mrs. Fleming was outside hanging sheets on the line when I got off the bus. She waved and told me to go ahead inside, and she would be there in a minute. I did not like that because I already knew I would not like Mr. Fleming.

I pushed the door open a little bit and stepped inside very quiet. I hoped Mr. Fleming would not be around until Mrs. Fleming finished hanging sheets and came inside. Only, he was sitting in the living room and he could see me from the chair he was in.

"You must be Bethany," he said.

"Yes."

"I'm Jerry Fleming," he said. "You can call me Jerry."

"I only say Mr. and Mrs. for grownups," I told him. "Mother says that is polite."

"All right then," he said. "Well, I'd best shake your hand if we're going to be formal for now."

Mr. Fleming pushed himself up and grabbed a crutch like Mira had one time when she twisted her ankle at a picnic. My eyes opened very wide when I saw why he needed it.

"You only have one leg!" I said, even though that was a rude thing to say. Sometimes if I am surprised, words come out by themselves.

"What?" Mr. Fleming said. "Are you sure?" He looked down at himself. "By golly, you're right! I *do* only have one leg."

Then he laughed, which made me laugh too. That was when I knew that I could not be cross at Mr. Fleming for living in Mrs. Goldsborough's house after all.

After Mrs. Fleming came in, we had gingersnaps and milk. Mr. Fleming told me about how he had two legs when he was younger but then he had to go away to fight in a war and one of his legs got blown to smithereens.

Mrs. Fleming told him to tone it down but I liked the way he told stories. Then Mrs. Fleming told me about how they had been friends when they were kids but then she had not seen him for years until she went back to her hometown for a visit.

"I'd always been crazy about her," Mr. Fleming said. "But I never thought I had a chance, especially after I lost my leg."

Mrs. Fleming smiled. "We spent a lot of time talking when I was home on that visit, but it wasn't until I was getting ready to leave that I realized I had fallen in love with Jerry."

"So she showed up at my door one day and when I opened it she said, 'I love you. Now what are you gonna do about it?'"

"What did you do?" I asked.

"I said, 'Call the preacher!' And I married her quick before she could change her mind."

It was the most romantic story I had ever heard.

Chapter Twenty

The day of our Weather Fair finally came! It had been a long wait because some of the students took so long finishing their projects. Mr. Wolnoth would not go ahead with the fair until every project was done. He said if we were going to represent all kinds of weather, we could not leave any out.

We pushed our desks to go around the school room in a big square but we left one place open at a corner. That was how we went in to stand behind our projects. Some of them took up more than their half of the desk even though Mr. Wolnoth had told us the biggest size they could be before we did them. It was lucky there were some smaller ones to give the big ones more room.

When the fair was happening, we had to stand behind our projects so people would know what we did. Also, if anyone had a question, we had to answer. I hoped no one would ask me something I did not know.

Before the fair started, we had a chance to look at all the other projects. It was very thrilling. I never saw so many kinds of weather before. Lots of the projects were very interesting. Lawrence Philpot's project was "Wind" and he had made a tree which was bent sideways. It looked real, except for a few places where you could see tape holding branches on.

My cousin Rose had "Rainbow". She told me she knitted it with different colours of yarn. A wire held the rainbow in place. I liked it even though it sagged in the middle, which a real rainbow does not do.

Luke Haliwell's desk was right next to Rose's because they are in the same grade. His project was built on a round piece of wood that turned like a merry-go-round when you pushed it with your finger. There was a mountain in the middle. One side of the mountain was covered with trees and bushes, but the other side was brown and rocky. I was looking at it when Luke came over and said, "You did a good job with the snow, Bethany."

"Thank you," I told him. "You did a good job with the green and brown mountain."

Luke smiled. He pointed to the brown side and said, "This is a rain shadow."

I looked harder. "Where is the shadow?" I asked.

"It's not a shadow like the sun makes," Luke said. "A rain shadow happens when a cloud is forced to empty all its rain on one side of a mountain, and there is nothing left for the other side."

Suddenly, it seemed as if I could hear Mira's voice in my ear, telling me she was the beautiful green side of the mountain and I was the rain shadow.

"It is true," I said. "I am like a rain shadow."

I did not mean to say it out loud. That happened by accident. Lucky for me, only Luke was close enough to hear me. He leaned down a little bit.

"What do you mean?" he asked.

"I was thinking about what my sister Mira would say." Then I told him how she liked to tell me that she was a jewel and I was a stone, or she was a rose and I was a cabbage. Luke frowned but he did not ask any other questions and I went to look at more of the projects.

Then Mr. Wolnoth said, "Students! It's time for us to open the doors to the public. Take your positions and look smart."

We all went and stood behind our projects. It was exciting when people started to come in. Everyone walked around the room and smiled at us and looked at all the projects.

I was happy when Daddy came. He said he was proud of me for doing such a fine job. I said I was proud of him too, so he would not think I forgot about the help he gave me.

Other people said things like, "Isn't that nice?" and "That looks just like snow," and "Good for you."

I said, "Thank you," to everyone, because that is polite.

Near the end of the Weather Fair, Mr. and Mrs. Fleming came in. I was surprised because they do not have any children. Then Mrs. Fleming pointed and said, "There she is!" and they came straight to me.

"Did you come to see my snow project?" I said.

"Of course," Mr. Fleming said.

"We wouldn't miss it for the world," Mrs. Fleming said.

They looked at it for a long time and talked about how much work it must have been and said what a wonderful job I did.

It was my favourite day I ever had of school. Even better than the day I read *Make Way for Ducklings*. Usually if there is a play or concert, I never get to do any of the fun parts, but everybody got to do the very same thing for the Weather Fair. I was exactly like the others.

After it was over, Mr. Wolnoth said we had done him proud and we should give ourselves a big hand. Then it was time to go home.

Except there was another surprise! When we got close to our house Daddy turned the car into the Fleming's driveway. We went inside.

Mrs. Fleming had made a coconut cake. She said it was the nearest thing she could think of to look like snow. Mr. Fleming said it was our own private Weather Fair celebration.

"I think we were almost as excited about the big event

as you were, Bethany," Mrs. Fleming said.

"Couldn't help it," Mr. Fleming said. "You've hardly talked about anything else in the month you've been coming here after school."

Daddy smiled a lot. When Mrs. Fleming asked me would I like a second piece of cake and I looked at Daddy to see if it was okay, he said it was so delicious it would be hard to only eat one.

I did not even want to fall to sleep that night! I wanted to stay awake to think about the Weather Fair and the party the Flemings had for me.

There was only one tiny thing that kept it from being perfect. I had something that belonged to Mrs. Fleming and she did not know I had taken it.

I knew I should have told her about it, but I was afraid.

Chapter Twenty-One

The Flemings did fun things with me every day after school. We made cookies and played games and they read me lots of stories and poems. Sometimes we went shopping or for a drive or to visit Mrs. Tait. But my favourite thing of all was playing dress-up.

Mrs. Fleming said I could put on anything I wanted from her closet. Dresses and hats and scarves. Even shoes.

She would take her jewellery box from the top of the dresser and put it on the bed.

"Accessorizing is very important," she would say.

The jewellery box was full of coloured beads and pretend pearls and diamonds. There were necklaces and bracelets and pins and rings. She always told me to pick anything I wanted.

Every time I got dressed up, I went downstairs and Mr. Fleming would say something like, "My dear, Mrs. Fleming! Why didn't you tell me we were having such a distinguished guest? I would have had the butler polish the good silver."

But the last time I played dress-up, I found out I had something that belonged to Mrs. Fleming. I saw it at the bottom of the box when I was putting a necklace away.

My face got hot and my heart started to thump. Also, I felt very confused.

Another secret.

I did not like keeping secrets. I was scared about what would happen if people found out. I tried not to think about them, only they kept coming into my head.

It was worse after the cake and party, because I had done something wrong to Mrs. Fleming and then she did something nice for me. It was very hard not to think about that the next day at school.

Mr. Wolnoth was not pleased with us that morning. He said we could not use the Weather Fair as an excuse to be rowdy. Also, he said if we did not settle down and stop making too much noise, we were not going to have recess. After that everyone behaved better because recess is the most fun part of the day.

Only, when it was time to go out for recess, Luke came over and said he had something to tell me about the rain shadow he made for his weather project. I went with him to where they were all lined up on the floor at the back of the room. He kneeled down so I kneeled down too.

"I forgot to show you this yesterday," he said. He pointed to little spots of green near the bottom of the brown side of the mountain.

"What are they?" I said.

"Those are plants. Not much can grow in a rain shadow, because it doesn't get rained on like the other side of the mountain," Luke said. "But see here? There are a few that can."

"That is not very interesting," I said. I did not like to think I was wasting my recess to hear that.

Luke laughed. "Maybe not," he said. "But the plants that grow on the rain shadow side are actually *stronger* than the ones that get lots of rain."

I felt something get still and quiet inside me, like I needed to listen very careful. Then Luke said another thing.

"They have to try harder to make it. These plants never give up."

"Like best effort," I whispered.

Luke smiled. "Yes, best effort. I think that makes them brave, too. They're strong and brave, *like you*."

Then I did not care about missing recess at all.

Even after Luke told me I was strong and brave, I needed two more days before I could tell Mrs. Fleming about the bad thing. I tried doing a practice in my head but it did not work because I did not know what Mrs. Fleming would say.

I did it right after school. As soon as I got there, Mrs. Fleming asked me what I would like to do.

"Can I see your jewellery box?" I asked.

She said I could and we went right straight to her room. I felt shaky inside but I made myself reach into the box, and then into my pocket, where I had put my half penny that morning.

My throat felt strange and tight and that made it hard to talk, so I just held out the two halves of the penny to Mrs. Fleming. Her eyes got big and round and her hand shook when she reached out to take them.

"Bethany," she said. Her voice was shaking just like her hand. "Where did you get this?"

I told her about how I picked it up when the girl named Gracie dropped it on the playground at school but that I did not mean to keep it. And I explained how I did not know it was Mrs. Fleming's until I saw the other half in her jewellery box.

"I promise, really and truly—I would never steal anything from you," I said.

"Of course you wouldn't," Mrs. Fleming said. She kept staring at the half of the penny I had just given back.

"I do not know how Gracie got it," I said after a moment.

Mrs. Fleming patted the bed beside her. I went and sat there.

"I assumed you knew this but I see now that you didn't. Bethany, I am Gracie's mother."

That did not make sense.

"But Gracie's mother is Raedine Moore," I said. "I heard people say her name lots of times."

Mrs. Fleming closed her eyes. She took a big breath and then opened them again.

"I *was* Raedine Moore," she said. "Until I married Jerry. Now I'm Raedine Fleming."

"Oh," I said. I thought about that for a minute. "I did not mean to take Gracie's penny."

"I know that, honey," Mrs. Fleming said. She smiled and put her arm around me and said, "This is one of those things that seems impossible—and yet it's happened. I don't know what it means, or if it means anything at all, but there's something wonderful about this."

"Because you have the other half of your penny back?" I asked.

"It feels like I have much more than that back," she said.

Chapter Twenty-Two

Doing hard things gets easier when you practice. After I told Mrs. Fleming about the penny, I felt brave and proud of myself. That is why I picked the very next day to tell Daddy the secrets I did not think I would ever say to him.

It was not easy to start. That made my voice sound croaky and strange.

"Daddy, I have three things to tell you that are bad. Secrets."

Daddy stopped washing dishes. He took the cloth for drying from me and wiped his hands. After that he pulled out two chairs at the table.

"Why don't we sit down and you can tell me everything," he said.

I told Daddy how sometimes I was afraid of Mother

and how part of me missed her but a different part of me did not really and truly mind that she did not come home. I said I was sorry about that part.

"No, *I'm* the one who's sorry, Bethany. I let you down because I didn't see how you were being affected by all of this. I should have been paying closer attention."

"That is okay, Daddy. It is not really your fault because I did not tell you the truth."

"What didn't you tell me the truth about?"

"The day Mother asked you why did Mira have to be the one who died, I pretended I did not hear that."

Daddy closed his eyes and put his head down for a minute before he answered.

"You must be tired of hearing that your mother was crazy with grief, but I need to say it again. Someday, she'll have to face the things she's done, and when that day comes, I hope you'll be able to forgive her."

"You should always forgive someone if they are really sorry for what they did," I said. Because that is something Mother used to tell me and Mira.

Daddy smiled. Then it was time to tell him the hardest secret. I took a big breath. When I started to talk I did not look at Daddy.

"The last secret is I let in the people who made Mira sick and that is why she died. Mother said if I did not do that Mira would still be here. Then everything would be the way it was before. I am so sorry, Daddy."

Then I looked up, because even though I was scared I had to see if Daddy was angry or if his eyes were looking at me the way Mother's had. As soon as I saw his face, I knew it was okay.

Daddy reached over and held my hand. He told me he was sad that I had been feeling that way.

Daddy told me I had not done anything wrong when I let the people into the house. He said if he or Mother or Mira had gone to the door, they would all have done exactly the same thing I did.

Daddy said Mother should not have said that to me because it was not true. He said she knew in her heart I had not done anything wrong. Then he told me we should try to forgive Mother because it is not good to carry around anger toward anyone.

"I will try," I said.

"And, from now on, I don't want you keeping things inside," he said. "If something troubles you, or worries you, or makes you feel bad in any way, I want you to come and tell me about it so I can help."

"You cannot help *everything*, Daddy," I said.

Daddy looked surprised. He said, "That's true, sweetheart. But, tell me, what kinds of things do you mean?"

I thought about that for a moment. One thing I like about Daddy is how he does not mind if I take my time to answer him when we are talking.

There are lots of things Daddy cannot do. When I was little I did not know that. I was surprised when rain spoiled our plans for a picnic one day, he could not do anything about the weather. And I hardly believed it when Daddy could not pick up a large rock Mother wanted to paint and put in her garden.

But those are not the kinds of things I was thinking about this time. I was thinking about the things he could not fix that would bring Mother back and make things the way they used to be.

"You cannot help *me*, Daddy," I said. "You cannot fix me and make me into a perfect girl like Mira."

Then Daddy got tears on his face.

"Bethany," he said, "I want you to listen very carefully to what I'm going to tell you."

I listened as hard as I could.

"You do not *need* to be fixed, sweetheart. You are not broken."

"But, Daddy—" I said. Then I did not say the rest because Daddy held his finger up, which means wait.

"Keep listening," Daddy said. "You are supposed to be *exactly* the way you are. If you were different, you would not be you."

"Who would I be?" I asked, very surprised.

"You would be somebody else. And that would be terrible."

"Even if the somebody else learned better, and did not have one short leg?"

"That would *not be you*," Daddy said. "God made you *who* you are by making you just the *way* you are."

I did not know what to say to that, but Daddy was not finished talking.

"Do you ever think about all the *good* things that are part of you?"

At first I did not know what Daddy meant. Then I remembered the time Mary said I was always kind and nice. Also, how I won Best Effort, and the way Mrs. Goldsborough loved to have me visit her. And I remembered that I am like a rain shadow where things that grow are brave and strong.

"But what about the parts that are *not* good?" I asked.

Daddy smiled. "*Everyone* has those too. Your friends, Lizzie and Mary, for example. Are they perfect?"

"No. Sometimes Mary tattles on the boys at school and Lizzie says cross things when she is grumpy. Those are not nice things to do."

"You see, honey," Daddy said. "Nobody is perfect. And that includes all of us—you and me and Mommy and Mira. But everybody is unique."

I did not know what unique was, but Daddy explained it means different.

"Imagine how boring the world would be if we were all exactly the same."

That did not sound good to me. I said, "I would not like it if Mary and Lizzie were not themselves."

"And *I* would not like it if *you* were not yourself," Daddy said. "You are special and wonderful just as you are."

I could not stay sitting on my chair then because I needed to hug Daddy. I hugged him the hardest I ever hugged anybody.

Epilogue

My birthday came last week. I thought it would feel different to be a teenager but it feels exactly like twelve.

I had a party at my house. It was on Saturday even though my birthday was on Tuesday. That was because Saturday was a better day for a party. I invited Mary Haig and Lizzie Newmarch and Lawrence Philpot and Luke Haliwell. Daddy said maybe I should include my cousins. I was not sure about that idea, but I called them on the telephone. Rose answered.

"Hello. This is Bethany," I said. "Do you and Kenny and Carl want to come to my party? For my birthday?"

"You want us to come to your birthday party?" Rose said. She sounded very surprised.

"Yes, please," I said. "My birthday is on Tuesday but the party is on Saturday."

"Well, thank you, Bethany," Rose said. "Of course, we would love to come. I'm so glad you invited us."

That made me feel happy. Daddy says family always loves you even if they do not show it sometimes, and I think he is right about that one.

Then Rose asked did I want her mom and dad to come too. I told her yes. Also, I invited the Flemings and Mrs. Melchyn and Daddy.

I did not invite Mrs. Goldsborough because she lives too far away. She sent me a card with a dollar in it anyway.

Everybody came except Lawrence because he had to help his father that day. But on Friday he said, "Happy birthday. I hope you have a great party," and he made his hands into fists with his thumbs pointed at the sky. I think that means good luck.

It was a wonderful party. We played a game called Musical Chairs four times. It was very fun even if I did not win. We wore triangle paper hats and ate hotdogs and potato chips. Then Daddy lit the candles on the cake and everybody sang Happy Birthday and I blew the candles out except three. Rose said that means I have three boyfriends, but that is not a Really and Truly. We had three-coloured ice cream with the cake. After that we went into the living room because it was time to open presents.

I got a game called checkers and a yo-yo and some

hair clips and a paint-by-numbers of a pony. I also got a nightgown and a yellow blouse.

The Flemings gave me a View-Master which was almost my favourite present. Except then Daddy went in the other room and came back with a box and when I looked inside I could hardly believe it.

It was a little gray kitten! Daddy said I could name him anything I liked, so I named him Bibs because it looks like he is wearing a white bib under his chin. Bibs is the best kitten in the world.

After the party was over and I said, "Thank you very much for coming" to everyone, all of my guests went home. That is when Daddy said there was one more present for me.

It was from Mother. The present Mother sent was called Mr. Potato Head. Mary Haig's brother has one and it is very fun to play with.

Mother also sent a letter which Daddy read to me. It said:

> Dear Bethany,
>
> How are you? I hope you are doing well. It is hard to believe you are already thirteen years old! I hope you have a lovely birthday and a great year ahead. I plan to come and see you during the summer, when I have my holidays from work. Until then, be good for Daddy.
>
> Love,
> Mom

Daddy said I should send a thank-you note to Mother. He helped me with the hard words and I wrote: "Dear Mother, I am fine. Thank you for the Mr. Potato Head. It is very nice. Love, Bethany."

Only, I wish I could write better to tell Mother more things than that. After I keep doing my best effort, I will be able to read and write more all by myself. Then I will do another letter for Mother. It will say:

> Dear Mother,
>
> It is me, your daughter Bethany. Probably you are surprised at how good I can write letters now. Did you know that I got a certificate at school? It was for never giving up. That is how I learned to write more and more words. Also, I read a whole book by myself. It was *Make Way for Ducklings* which Mira gave to me after she did not want it anymore.
>
> I hope you are doing good and that you like your job and that the place you live is nice. I hope you are not sad all the time anymore.
>
> Daddy can make lots of things for supper now. I help him. Some of our meals are not so good but some are almost good like yours. Only, we do not know how to make casseroles yet. If we have leftovers, we just heat them in the frying pan.
>
> There are new neighbours in Mrs. Goldsborough's house. Only, it is their house now. Their names are Raedine and Jerry Fleming, only I call them Mr. and Mrs. Fleming. I go there after school until Daddy comes home from work. Daddy says they are a god-

send, which means we are lucky to have them.

I have a new kitten named Bibs. He is gray, not orange like Maxwell. Also, he is only small but he will grow bigger.

Do you know what a rain shadow is, Mother? I learned about that kind of weather when we had our Weather Fair at school. It was not my project but the boy who did that project told me about them. One side of the mountain is green with trees and plants and the other side is brown but it is all part of the same mountain. Hardly anything can grow on the brown side but the plants that are there are very strong.

Daddy says maybe you will come home someday. He says you might realize you are just as unhappy there as you were here. I do not think that is a good reason. I think you should pick the place where you are happy.

Love,
Bethany

Acknowledgements

With thanks to Christie Harkin and Cheryl Chen for their excellent editorial guidance. It is a pleasure and a privilege to work with people who connect so well with a story.

Thanks also to the readers in kidcrit who cheered me on in the early stages of writing this book.

And, of course, to my husband Brent and my family and friends, for all they are and do.

I acknowledge, with thanks, the support of the Canada Council for the Arts, which last year invested $157 million to bring the arts to Canadians throughout the country.

Je remercie le Conseil des arts du Canada de son soutien. L'an dernier, le Conseil a investi 157 millions de dollars pour mettre de l'art dans la vie des Canadiennes et des Canadiens de tout le pays.

Also by Valerie Sherrard

Tumbleweed Skies
978-1-55455-113-2 • $12.95

- 2010 Booklist Editors' Choice book
- 2010 Ann Connor Brimer Award for Children's Literature Nominee

A motherless girl, a grandmother who cannot forgive, an injured magpie and a warm prairie summer.

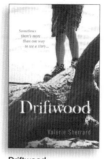

Driftwood
978-1-55455-305-1 • $9.95

- 2014 CLA Book of the Year for Children Award nominee
- 2015 Rocky Mountain Book Award nominee

An angry boy's summer. Endings and beginnings and encounters with an old man and his magical tales.

The Glory Wind
978-1-55455-170-5 • $12.95

- 2011 Ann Connor Brimer Award for Children's Literature winner
- 2011 Geoffrey Bilson Award for Historical Fiction for Young People winner
- 2012 Silver Birch Fiction Award nominee
- 2011 TD Canadian Children's Literature Award nominee
- 2011 CLA Book of the Year for Children Award nominee

A friendship that should have been perfect...until whispers spoke of a shameful secret.

Valerie's Teen Read

Counting Back from Nine
978-1-55455-245-0 • $9.95

- 2013 Governor General's Literary Award finalist
- 2014 Forest of Reading's Red Maple-Fiction nominee
- 2013 Ontario Library Association Best Bets List Honourable Mention

Bethany knows that she is special. She doesn't learn things as easily as her classmates do and that sometimes makes them mean to her. They call her names—including the really "bad" name. Even her mom and her sister Mira say unkind things at times. But Bethany has friends like her neighbour Mrs. Goldsborough as well as happy times with Daddy when he gets home from work. And now, Mira has promised to protect her from the bullies when the new school year begins.

Then tragedy strikes, tearing Bethany's world apart in ways she could never have imagined, and she starts to wonder if there will ever be a place that feels like home again.

Award-winning author Valerie Sherrard revisits the world of *The Glory Wind* in her new historical novel.

Born in Moose Jaw, Saskatchewan, Valerie Sherrard has written a number of books for young readers including *Tumbleweed Skies*, *Counting Back from Nine*, *Driftwood*, and the award-winning *Glory Wind*. She lives in New Brunswick.

Fitzhenry & Whiteside
www.fitzhenry.ca

$12.95
ISBN 978-1-55455-341-9

9 781554 553419

51295>